Algernon Gissing

The Sport of Stars

Vol. 1

Algernon Gissing

The Sport of Stars
Vol. 1

ISBN/EAN: 9783337411909

Printed in Europe, USA, Canada, Australia, Japan

Cover: Foto ©Andreas Hilbeck / pixelio.de

More available books at **www.hansebooks.com**

THE SPORT OF STARS

BY

ALGERNON GISSING

AUTHOR OF

'A MOORLAND IDYL,' 'A VILLAGE HAMPDEN,' ETC.

IN TWO VOLUMES.

VOL. I.

LONDON:

HURST AND BLACKETT, LIMITED,

13, GREAT MARLBOROUGH STREET.

1896.

All Rights Reserved.

THE SPORT OF STARS.

CHAPTER I.

THE ONE TOO MANY.

'GOT it, Ben?'

'I've got it, Leah.' And Saloway rose from his chair deliberately, taking up a standing position before his wife.

She, anxious for the outcome of a long and fervent deliberation, gazed at him with lips apart, letting her hands and sewing fall into her lap.

'I've got it, Leah,' the man repeated, in a tone of firmer conviction, 'and I don't see as any mortal can gainsay it. I shall take 'em to the squire in the morning, that be the upshot of the matter. Let he make of it what seem good to 'n. It be "The Peasant's Warning Voice" as I stand upon, and it do seem to I as what be fit for folks in other parishes be as fit for we here in Win'ol.'

The wife looked silently into her husband's face, until he, saying that he would just go up street to tell 'em, took his hat and went out, leaving Leah to transfer her gaze to the few white wood embers in the grate.

It was the night of the 3rd of August, 1849, and in Winwold this young energetic cobbler, Benjamin Saloway by name, had been contemplating the social outlook, as some at that time did here and there with seriousness of a grim kind. This man did not come of a demonstrative race, but the fire of his present enthusiasm was not to be hidden. For some time he had been engaged with it, now it clamoured for a definite solution.

As Saloway stepped into the darkness, the wind moaned over the wooded slopes that surrounded this remote village, and handfuls of rain were flung from the low scudding clouds. The street was wide and the houses scattered, the only lights being those which appeared in cottage windows, upon the blinds whereof was printed the shadows of geraniums, and here and there of a magnified head and shoulders. Benjamin gave these conditions but a casual glance as, pulling his coat about him, he strode hastily along the road.

The cottage before which he stopped was at the extreme verge of the village, just where the road began its wooded ascent of the hill beyond; and from which realm of darkness and mystery there came at this moment on the rain the weird halloo of a restless owl. As this touched the cobbler's ears, he knocked and entered.

'Be John at whum?'

'That be Ben's voice, I count.'

'Ult come in the morning, John?' said the visitor, with a singular impulsiveness, as he blinked at the candle-light. 'I can't be off it.'

He was bidden be seated, and John Parish, removing the pipe from his mouth, was about to adjust himself to a leisurely discussion. But

Saloway did not sit, and showed continued signs of anything but leisure.

'I thought of you, John, Joseph Leman, Richard and Henry Claydon, Ralph Strange, and me. We be quiet, tidy men, I judges, as any in the country, and as nobody can say a word against. We shall conduct ourselves quite respectful, of course. I be'nt for they as go with violence nohow.'

'Ne'er a bit, Benjamin. I be ready to go sure enough, and quite peaceable an' all.'

'We'll ask he for a bit of land at the same rent as Farmer Righton's, to raise our bread and 'tatoes, do you see, to give we employment when there be no work, and to keep we from the public-house and the parish in the winter.'

'That be the item, Ben. A be a rum 'un by all accounts, but we'll speak him fair.'

'Come at ten o'clock in the morning, John, by the gate in Upper Marbrook.'

'That I 'ull; but look 'e, Ben——'

Hearing the door click, John looked up from the fire in the middle of his sentence, and Saloway was no longer there.

'Well, Benjamin,' mused the astonished wagoner, who was now alone, 'you be a rum 'un yourself an' all; but I'll go, o' course.'

And John Parish again lapsed into the healthy oblivion of the odd moments of a countryman.

The cobbler flitted through the wet night to the several houses, leaving with each the same brief summons and the same measure of astonishment at his singular appearance and behaviour. Unwonted action of necessity destroyed the somnolent balance in such as Saloway, and he found it impossible to be still in one place for many consecutive moments. The conversation and society of his comrades would have seemed to offer a refuge from this nervous state, but he found it to be otherwise. His vital announcement once made, he found it impossible to talk to them. He must be alone. The unruly night was fittest companion for him. Even from his own fire-side,—but perhaps rather from the timid gaze of his Leah,—he shrank. He passed his door, and went on into the solitary road beyond it, pacing or standing beneath the trees, amongst the dark branches of which the rain and the wind made mournful music.

It was nearing midnight when the man, slinking into the flickering candle-light, disturbed his wife's unquiet slumbers. He would speak but little; but when summoned to the table he ate ravenously.

The following morning broke exquisitely fair, with a brisk north-west wind, and a drenched earth sparkling to the stare of the sun. The atmosphere was transparent as crystal, and the invigorating breeze which danced from a clear blue horizon seemed to invite to exceptional enterprise. Ten o'clock was known to be the hour at which the young squire would tolerate approaches from any of his dependents, so that some half-hour before that time the six chosen representatives of the labourers of Winwold could be seen crossing the sunny pastures which lay between the village and the Hall. The 'wambling' gait of the men seemed unusually conspicuous, owing no doubt to the assumption of Sunday garments for an occasion which was secular. The men or their clothes were uncomfortably impressed with the fact of the incongruity. To add to it they were preternaturally silent, scarcely half-a-dozen words being exchanged on the way, and these with but independent reference to the state of the ' lattermath ' which the near fields presented, or of the harvest which was proceeding farther off. They all looked for the most part to the ground, taking a general expression from the unusual solidity of their leader Saloway.

When they came to the back premises of the Hall, there were sounds in the stable-yard, and, finding the opportunity favourable, Benjamin stepped in to inquire of the groom his master's whereabouts. To the cobbler's visible discomfiture, he confronted that master in person, who, with the groom beside him, was handling a new bit which glistened like silver.

' Hulloa !' cried Mr. Blakenhurst, scanning the intruder, and thinking him alone. 'Saloway? Do you want me ?'

Mr. Geoffrey Blakenhurst was in those days a handsome man of but three or four years over thirty, but, as he had inherited early, his magisterial character was by now familiar to his world. Stepping forward, his eye encountered the figures of Benjamin's companions, and his brow clouded.

'What do you want?' he asked, keeping his eyes upon the regiment, and, as the members of it did not doubt, making a mental note of the names of every one of them.

The popular unrest of those days is matter of history with which we need not now deal. With positive violence did the plough-workers, like others, clamour for more tolerable conditions of life, and the extreme measures were the means of disseminating some amount of theory amongst those who were principally affected, and in places it found abiding soil. Amongst other things, out in the fields the cry for allotments went up,—for small plots of land, that is, which the labourer was to hold as strictly supplementary to his daily labour, and at admittedly disproportionate rental. In some districts the suggestion found ready favour; in others, that such a preposterous demand could claim even a show of plausibility, not to speak of reason, was as vigorously contested. The status of such opposition district was, however, one of intellectual dignity compared with that of a place like Winwold during the supremacy of Mr. Geoffrey Blakenhurst. The former brandished some species of argument; the latter declined to make use of any such degenerate weapon.

Upon most subjects Mr. Blakenhurst personally loathed argument; upon such an elementary postulate as this one it put him into a frenzy. He conceived the world as of several clearly defined circles or galleries. What he conceived, he enunciated; and what in the name of first principles had argument to do in such a matter?

Saloway had already made 'his obedience,' as he himself would have termed the ordinary display of social deference, and now the rest doffed their caps humbly.

'We wish to speak to you, sir, if you please,' returned the young cobbler, suddenly awaking to the fact that he had undertaken to bear the brunt of the encounter.

'Certainly you can speak to me.' The squire

took his watch from his pocket as he said this. 'Go ahead.'

'I beg your pardon, sir,' said Saloway. 'We should have had no thought of intruding, had us known it would be inconvenient to you. If you would rather as we came at——'

Mr. Blakenhurst laughed, and asked him if he thought he could be bothered twice, ending with a colloquial injunction to him to proceed. Gathering a momentary courage from the unaccommodating reception, Saloway did proceed.

'I doubt we can't dispose of it all in a minute, sir. I was hopeful as you might be at leisure to talk over with we the subject of allotments, being as they have received a deal of attention in many parts of late, and as it do seem clearly proved that they be of uncommon benefit to poor labourers who don't work half their time, such as be the case with a many in Win'ol at this minute.'

Saloway delivered this sentence with unusual speed, as though afraid of interruption before getting the preliminaries stated, and as, in truth, the squire's countenance betrayed scant appreciation of the impending discussion.

'You want to talk about allotments, do you? . . . Allotments, is it? And who has been putting you up to that, eh? . . . Who? . . . Tell me, Saloway, for you seem to be the ringleader in the conspiracy. Who has been preaching these revolutionary doctrines in my peaceful parish? Speak, and don't stand there like a sturdy sheep, you blockhead.'

'I be no man for revolutionary doctrines, Squire Blakenhurst, as you know as well as I do myself. We only come here respectful, like honest, sober men, to talk with you, who be our natural master, concerning our grievances——'

'Grievances!' roared the squire, mirthfully. 'Who the devil told you that you'd got any grievances? Where did you pick the word up, I'd like to know? It's we that have the grievances, I can tell you, for here are six of you lazy blackguards come blathering here about things you don't understand at ten o'clock of a fine morning, when you might be earning a pound a week by cutting all that corn of ours waiting for harvest. Go about your business; and if you, Saloway, don't want to end your days on the gallows, I should recommend you to get rid of all this revolutionary trash about grievances and allotments. You're at the head of this affair, I see, and I won't have it brought into my parish, do you hear?'

'These may be your opinions now, sir,' returned Benjamin, with surprising readiness, 'but if you'd just give a look into things I be quite sure as you'd think differently. It be'nt my place to take it upon me to argue with you, but if I might be so bold as beg you to read this little book which I shall be glad to lend to you, written by a man as be no enemy to his country, landlords or labourers alike, and that is John Denson of Waterbeach, called by title "The Peasant's Warning Voice to Landlords"——'

'What are you talking about to me, you scoundrel!' cried the squire, at last genuinely incensed by the man's impudence and pertinacity. 'You've got blasphemous and seditious books, have you? You're no friend to revolution, and yet you threaten me with warning voices, do you? You'll be burning my ricks, or shooting me from behind a hedge, I suppose? It isn't enough that I've to pay hundreds a-year to feed a lot of d——d idle paupers like you, is it, but you must come here to threaten my life if I don't give you my best land to fatten on. Very good; I refuse, I tell you, and I can tell you further that the first man who tries to carry out the threats you speak of will be a dead man. I am ready for you, and can defend myself,'— Mr. Blakenhurst actually did produce a pistol from some mysterious pocket at the back of his trousers—'so I give you notice.'

Saloway looked into the squire's face, but uttered no other word. As he turned, crest-fallen, to follow his companions, who had shrunk away several sentences ago, it was doubtful if he heard the ringing laugh of mockery which a woodpecker flung him from the great elm-tree on the slope behind. The squire had worked himself into such a rage that he also retreated to the house without another word.

The result of the cobbler's experiment was quickly noised abroad, as of course the inception of it had also been, and sullen faces shook over the conviction that 'no good 'ud come of it.'   It seemed to be accepted as final, it occurring to nobody to repeat the attempt. The squire doubtless knew his public, and his victory was supreme. The energetic young cobbler, moreover, inevitably came in for much of the discontent and discredit which, in Winwold as elsewhere, signal failure of necessity aroused.   The scheme was now attributed wholly to him, the boldness and the miscarriage of it.   In the daily expectation of some personal disaster to follow the squire's violent displeasure, the five voluntary associates of Benjamin on his ill-fated journey were not at all sure that they had ever desired allotments. But, happily, Mr. Blakenhurst had accurately singled out the ringleader.

Saloway was scarcely robust enough to sustain the whole odium of the misadventure. The personal disappointment was in itself punishment enough for him; for he had worked himself to such a pitch of fanaticism upon the subject that the blow came like a frustration of life itself. It was said that he was growing melancholy, and it could not be doubted that he never appeared in places of common resort. Most of his time was devoted to his trade, and if he went beyond his threshold it was invariably at night. The neighbours would question his wife about him, but Leah was as puzzled as the rest. One night, early in October, she received her first glimpse of enlightenment.

It was about nine o'clock, and Leah sat alone in her cottage expecting her husband's return. He was generally in by half-past eight. But, as to-night was exceptionally fine, she as yet thought little of it. The neighbour who had spent the evening in gossip with her had but recently gone, and had left her in good spirits. So the clock struck. After that, sitting so silently in her chair, with only the clock pendulum to keep her company, she dozed. The cottage door opened suddenly and disturbed her, when Leah, looking instinctively to the dial, found that it was nearly ten.

'Why, Ben, how late you be,' she said rubbing her eyelids, then saw that it was not her husband who had entered.

'So your husband beunt at home, missis?' said the intruder, whom Leah now recognized as a new under-keeper of the squire's.

'No, he've gone out as nsual. Most in general he be back before this. It be nearly ten o'clock.'

'It be,' said the youth, with a note of sarcasm. 'And a fine night for a walk. Good-night.'

As the man withdrew, a sickening fear came upon the lonely woman. She sped to the door, and called out through the dark,

'Have you seen my husband?'

'Oh ay, they'll have him by now,' was the jocular response.

Leah reeled as from an actual blow, and slunk again into her cottage. But the silence and the solitude were intolerable. She snatched down her white linen bonnet from its peg on the door, and went out. Still the stars and the dark tree outlines, held only by the whispering night breezes. When she had taken half a dozen steps from her doorway, a figure approached through the dark.

'Is that you, Ben?' the woman almost screamed.

'No, Leah, it be John Parish. I was a-coming to tell you as they've got Ben locked up for poaching.'

'Locked up! But—John, a never did such a thing in his life,' cried the distracted woman.

' That were my version of it,' the man replied, ' but they've took he none the less. It do all come of Ben's mooching about i' the dark, do you see, Leah? But don't 'e be affrighted, 'oman, it'll come right after a bit. However, I thought as you better know, you might have sat up all night for he else.'

'Oh, John——'

'Ay, ay,' said the man, kindly. 'It be uncommon ockard for you, that's certain. I cannot think what Ben be about in letting his head into such a maunder. But it'll come right arter a bit, never fear.'

Unable to sustain her part any further, Leah shrank back into the darkness, and heard the man's good-night without being able to give articulate response. Leah did sit up for her

husband throughout the night, despite the kindly intentions of her neighbour. Daylight proved
the report quite accurate. With every appearance of irresistible circumstance Saloway had
been taken, and was in custody to await his
trial. That there had lately been marauders
amongst the squire's game was matter of common gossip, but that the fanatical cobbler was
the instigator of these lawless practices had
never been even remotely suspected by his most
intimate acquaintance, until this skilful capture
of him, so to speak, red-handed. His nocturnal
wanderings became at once of course intelligible
to everyone. It was true, he had not the impli-
ments of his nefarious trade about him when he
was taken, nor any *corpus delicti* in his possession, but it was not difficult to surmise that he
was too shrewd a hand for that. The squire's
keepers had for some weeks had their suspicions
against him, and upon this particular evening,
after a skilful routing of a determined gang,
Benjamin was caught in full flight homewards,
everyone of his associates having unfortunately
effected their escape.

Before the criminal was removed from the village, he was allowed an interview with his wife. The desperate calamity gave Leah unwonted strength.

'It'll come right, Ben,' she affirmed, whilst gripping her husband's hand, ' you never did it, let 'em say what they will.'

Saloway was gloomy and undemonstrative. At the moment of parting, he clutched his wife.

'I never went a-poaching in my life, Leah, never,' twice he bitterly asserted. 'But—but they'll send me to Gloucester—I know 'em will.' And then his voice failed him.

The cobbler's presentiments proved well founded. Much went to substantiate the charge against him; in fact, as at Quarter Sessions it was ultimately decided, to put his guilt beyond any reasonable doubt. In view of the evidence given, the man was a dangerous one, from whom so secluded a district must have ample protection. In those times of social unsettlement, so the chairman cogently remarked, the duty of the magistracy was a clear one, however irksome or unpleasant. The country must be protected from the unprincipled bands of fanatics rising up in all directions, who seemed to find a strong religious virtue in subverting the order of the universe, and promoting a popular disregard of the laws of the realm. In country places this crime of poaching was one of the commonest manifestations of the evil spirit he had referred to, and as it was one fraught with the gravest danger to the community, frequently leading to riots and loss of life, the law had properly placed very considerable powers in the hands of the court, which it was their duty to exercise firmly. Although it was this prisoner's first proved offence, in face of the dangerous character incidentally revealed by it, the court would consider itself remiss in its duty to society at large, if it passed a smaller sentence than that of detention in Gloucester gaol for six months with hard labour. The newspaper reports of the time added, that after hearing the sentence the prisoner had to be assisted from the dock.

It was in the sunlight of the following spring, that a pale-faced silent man flitted like a ghost through Winwold, to be seen of several, but only to become thenceforth a mere traditional rumour and a tale. A day or two before his passing, this spectre's wife,—for alas, he had a woman that still clung to him,—received a letter in which, as in the midst of a consuming fire, these words were stamped, ' Only one night in Winwold, then we'll go to Millington where nobody will know us.'

Saloway came in by the lower road, and left by that which went by the Upton Quarry, passing beneath a row of beech-trees which bounded the parish at its eastern side. The sun shone down on him from a cloudless sky.

CHAPTER II.

IN EXILE.

SINCE Saloway's youth, increasing numbers have become the victims of that irresistible influence urging to the new, constantly present in the rational existence, but of action impulsive and intermittent, whereby 'the old woe o' the world' is periodically promoted, and through which now, for close on a century, man's soul's wings have been kept feverishly unfurled. Between such victims, however, and the serious cobbler of Winwold there was but little in common. They seek their new voluntarily, and, as may be supposed, find recompense sufficient in the uncertainty of the issue: the highest flight ever intended by Benjamin was pitifully short and definite.

Banishment from a homely soil, wherein all his habits and aims were deeply rooted, had formed no part of his plan; through none of the instinctive forces was he driven from the primrose path of the sunlit village to the dark and arid ways of a large industrial centre. The temperament of the 'revolutionary cobbler,' as the Winwold squire henceforth invariably called this insignificant antagonist, was simple in the extreme; a simplicity which proclaimed his incompetence for the modest enterprise he had taken in hand. But a small degree of complexity would have sufficiently equipped him, and by bringing the squire's life, or even his ricks, into the account, would have afforded Saloway more solid and worthy ground for the assumption of the martyr's crown.

For no uneven path was Benjamin made. He lacked hopelessly the pugnacious virtues. A staggering blow, instead of arousing all that was ferocious in him, and giving frantic strength to the excited energies, extinguished all the spirit he owned, and sent him off to fret his bruised soul in deepest retirement. This pusillanimity, (as our Christian ethics commonly adjudge it,) drove Saloway to the town, for even he seemed to be aware that no such effectual annihilation could be elsewhere presented. He needed this burial from himself as much as from his neighbours, so that mere exchange of a rural state would by no means have been to his mind.

For several years Benjamin Saloway steadily sank, until, short of crime, he sounded the lowest depths that a highly civilised existence can offer. From the cobbler of breezy Winwold, he in short developed into a cog in the Millington wheel, merging what might remain of a once fairly definite personality in the hopelessly inanimate toil of this inexorable engine of man's greed.

His wife Leah had soon succumbed to the altered conditions of life, somewhat earlier perhaps than need have been, on account of the feeble spark that remained to her being at that moment claimed for the continuance of her kind.

She died, bequeathing for her sole legacy a baby girl. The child lived, and Saloway's lowest point had been reached.

Throughout all his hours of toil, the child lay at his feet in a rude cradle made of a grocer's box, either watching in open-eyed bewilderment the dumb pantomime of the nimble fingers, or sleeping in still profounder indifference to the alien world into which she had come. Saloway was an object of ready sympathy to his neighbours, and a regular recipient of those numberless acts of benevolence upon which intercourse, nay, life itself, in that dingy world is so largely founded. Doubtless, without it the man's task would have found an end, for out of his trade he was by no means what women call a handy man.

The struggle for mere bread continued as severe as ever, but by a week of untold hours Saloway managed to supply his child with adequate provision; to what his own demands had fallen it is unnecessary to inquire. His Emily grew and prospered, and it had come that in this fact the whole of Benjamin's life was centred. He watched, and even taught her with unwearying care, thinking only of what could minister to her comfort or development. Penny toys he bought her, and he made a whole alphabet for her instruction out of odds and ends of leather which were useless in his work. The child showed a bright intelligence, and could read when she was five. Then began the cobbler's soul to revive within him. He would snatch half-an-hour to seek the nearest bookstall, and return triumphantly with some tattered volume. As he worked through the days that followed, he got a glimpse of a world beyond him, through the slowly articulated spellings of the little maiden planted on the floor by his side. In this way whole books were read, amongst them being the inevitable Bunyan, a volume of Josephus, and the 'Story of the Robins.'

But this very development of his child, profoundly as it encouraged the man, was at times as profound a source of depression. The impossibility of a moment's respite from the hourly grind presented its tragic stare, and through it all that green and flowery world from which

these little feet were so rigorously excluded.
Saloway felt that spectral problems began daily
to gather about him. Any thought of a return
to country scenes unnerved him still, but was
he for that to condemn an independent soul to
what his homely instincts felt to be an unnatural
fate? Emily had never known the freedom of
the fields and lanes, to be sure, but the cobbler
could draw no casuistical distinctions. Was it
not a source of shame and bitterness to himself
that she never had?

These questions assailed him with merciless
frequency, but the child was nearing seven years
old before Benjamin found strength to face the
inevitable.

One morning Emily awoke, and instead of
seeing the figure of her father bent over his
work, she saw him at the table with a book.
Aware of her movement, Saloway looked into
the small, inquiring face, and quailed before the
mute gaze of astonishment.

'Not at work, father?' said the child, with
precocious directness.

'It be Sunday,' was the man's reply.

'When people go to church? I thought you couldn't afford to know Sunday, father.'

'I be a-going to try, maidie. I must get it into the week somehow.'

It was not that Saloway had adopted any heterodox opinions in the course of his experiences; his life, like that of millions, was ordered solely by material stress.

'You have never seen the country as God made, Emily. We be going there to-day.'

Benjamin's decision was an heroic one, and it had been heroically come to. It was now physically as well as mentally painful to the cobbler to emerge into the light of day. His brain and eyeballs were seared by every sunbeam, just as positively as if he had been an owl or other bird of twilight. Yet as he turned the corner of his own dingy by-way into the sunlight of a broader thoroughfare, a sensation not wholly of pain swept over him. A breath of wind from a free inspiring world found its way to his withered heart, and for an instant revivified it, swelling all the chords to their natural suppleness and depth of sonorous tone.

But it passed quickly on its way, leaving behind but a desolate sough in the quivering frame through which it had flitted.

With Emily it was very different. This first adventure into an unknown world was like another birth to her; a first awakening to an enchanted reality of which she had vaguely heard, but not as yet even dimly seen. In the silence of the Sunday morning and high sunlight of early May, the very stones seemed to her transformed, to have acquired a glitter to heart and eye, and to the foot an elasticity of which she had never dreamed. Her colourless cheeks flushed, and her bright eyes darted hither and thither in speechless ecstacy. The world was not less, but so infinitely more brilliant than she had ever imagined it.

After an hour's walk, they reached the outskirts of the town; where the streets were, at any rate, broken, and bits of garden were allotted to the various houses. They passed a place where a house was building; a structure boarded and scaffolded, with an open gap between itself and its tenanted neighbour,—one of those gaps already sentenced, whereon foundation refuse, brick ends, tins, necks of bottles, and promiscuous filth of every kind defile the surface of its natural green. Saloway paused to examine the new building, in confused pre-occupation, then summoned Emily, who was behind. She was upon all fours, on what had once been grass, and heard him not. Nay, was she not eating that soiled and grimy herbage? The father turned quickly away under the grip of intolerable emotion. When the child rejoined him, she brandished something in her hand.

'As many as you like, Emily; 'em be only weeds.'

There were but daisies, dandelions, a buttercup or two, and colts'-foots, but in the child's fingers these despised little weeds acquired a depth of sanctity which could outweigh a whole world of ancient scorn. Saloway even saw this, and it aroused a painful contest in his disordered soul which he was in no condition just then to cope with. The effect of the flowers, those which grew upon the very road before his door in the old days, was, at opposite extremes, little less to him than to the new-born Emily. To her they could but bring a waft from an enchanted world now first disclosed, opening with untold brilliance into a whole infinity beyond, in the dazzling light of which lay screened a universe of hope and joy. To him they spoke of a world gone by, whereon the sun had set in lurid haze never to rise again. It was only these sunset hues which could be presented to him now, but in his daughter's eyes he saw the dawn, and the glimpse of it dismayed him.

A long day they made of it, advancing even to dishevelled hedge-rows, which enclosed spacious fields whereon only as yet appeared the builder's threat that, occasion fitting, they were ripe for the progressive scourge. Emily got more flowers, and was distressed that they should wither in her hand. Her father told her they would live again at home in water, so privately she sucked them, but not liking their flavour she had to give it up. The day was fine and warm throughout, and it was evening before, exhausted but reluctant, they reached the squalid shelter known to them as home.

'Shall we ever go again, father?' asked the child, through her burden of fatigue.

'Every Sunday when it be fine,' replied the man, with a courage which might not have been suspected.

The cobbler kept his word. Regularly, as Sunday morning came, the pair could be seen starting on their Sabbath journey, the child in irrepressible glee, the man in what appeared a faint haze of increased contentment. A few weeks' practice largely diminished the amount of strength expended, and the effect of the day's expedition upon their health was very soon apparent. So satisfactory had the experiment proved, that Benjamin could confront his sordid lot with a remarkable accession of tolerance. He found even a stimulus in the ceaseless prattle of the child, now based exclusively upon these Sunday walks, backward or to come, and it enabled him to widen considerably the range of his vision. Yet was the man's extended outlook exclusively on behalf of the child. His suffering from a sense of fear or crippling exposure upon passing the limits of his den continued as acute as ever.

One Sunday, early in July this time, when their walk had taken them in a fresh direction, they came to a region widely appropriated to market gardens, and the long rows of fruit-trees, with vast patches of vegetables in between, offered a spectacle novel and interesting to them both. It chanced that a public path ran through the centre of such a space, and intense was the delight with which they scanned the acres of lettuce, onions, and cabbages spread around, any single plant of which would have been a particular dainty in their restricted diet. The strawberries, raspberries, and currants scarcely raised an emotion in them, so hopelessly were they removed from any practical thought.

As they wandered slowly on, constantly detained by some new and startling revelation of the incredible bounty of the land, they came to a wide open sweep covered with a disordered growth which presented a striking contrast to the symmetry and regularity of the parts they had already passed.   Both father and daughter stared, but, as it chanced, with totally different reflections.

' What are they, father ?'

' Peas,' said Saloway, when the question had been twice repeated.

' Pea-pickers wanted.   Apply to——'
Emily read out the words thoughtlessly from a board erected a yard or two from the path.

'That be just the item,' mused the other. ' Would you like to come here all day, Emily, and pick the peas?' he asked at length, impulsively, and almost in a whisper.

' All day—on Sunday ?'

'No, no, maidie.   To-morrow—and Tuesday —and Wednesday, maybe.'

Their eyes met, and Benjamin resolved.

Again Saloway proved equal to the resolution, and the following morning he and Emily appeared amidst the ragged company which the sniff of an hour's open-air employment had gathered to the spot.   After a few explanatory words with the overlooker, who, with his weighing-machine, stood by an empty cart at one end of the field, the timorous pair was drafted to a station on the ground. It happened that, as Benjamin and the child entered, they had passed a woman, by appearance wretchedly poor and weak, who, with a boy by her side, had been evidently intent upon gaining a place in the employment of the day. So eager had the cobbler been to secure this coveted 'leave to toil,' upon which the day's sustenance very literally depended, that anything resembling the finer. feelings was sunk in the inevitable greed. Having passed, however, and been accepted, the figure of that woman again occurred to him, and a sensitive regret for what he now construed as a brutal outstripping of her feebler efforts, suddenly came over him. From his place, therefore, he cast anxious glances towards the point whence all must issue, and it was with a sense of positive relief that he saw the tattered object of his scruples, with that boy at her skirts, wending slowly over the field towards him. Conscience thus satisfied,

Benjamin and Emily set feverishly to work.

It broke into a hot and cloudless day, and no doubt the scene lacked not certain obvious elements pleasing to the fanciful idyllic sense. Incontestable was the fact that here lay a handful of perspiring mortals under the direct eye of heaven, passing at least through their hands a weft of that mysterious texture which cannot be mistaken for the work of man.

The peas picked were flung into a sack, and the joint exertions of the cobbler and his child soon sufficed to fill the one they had. When it could hold no more, Benjamin tied up the mouth and took his burden to be weighed, emptied, and paid for by the taskmaster. This was the man's duty for the day so long as daylight lasted.

It chanced that, from the place he occupied, Saloway commanded a near view of that woman and boy to whom his attention had before been momentarily given. As the cobbler went up with his third sack too, the diminutive boy toiled along under his first, and the opportunity of rendering a trivial service did not escape

Benjamin. After that he was constrained to watch more and more closely the noticeable pair. Simple as the work was, the woman sat frequently with idle hands in what seemed listless indifference to the occupation. The boy, too, was physically weak, but showed through his shabby clothing glimpses of incongruous intelligence and refinement. After that helpful encounter he returned Saloway's glances from time to time, and to his childish extent seemed to reciprocate the interest extended to him. If he made any attempt to engage his mother in the same diversion, his efforts must have been unavailing, for she betrayed not the smallest consciousness of the cobbler's or anybody else's existence about her.

Presently Saloway wiped his forehead with his shirt-sleeve, and paused in his work.

'Emily,' said he, 'it be my opinion as that woman be'nt well. Her can't work solid like we. What do you say to helping her a bit?'

The child was timid, but in view of the close proximity to her father she easily gave in to him, and Benjamin went to the woman's side.

The boy showed a gleeful acceptance of the arrangement in which his mother could but acquiesce in listless astonishment.

'Have a race with he, Emily,' said the cobbler, as he withdrew, 'and see who can pick most. I be'nt afar off.'

Emily's new companion was an intelligent, half-fed boy of eleven years old. Despite this difference of four years in their ages, they quickly discovered a marked compatibility of temperament, and in half-an-hour they advanced to the stage of a lifelong intimacy. As they picked, picked, at the bloom-tinted pea-pods incessantly, their tongues kept up a ceaseless accompaniment to their fingers. With the consummate frankness of childhood, they quickly revealed all the dark secrets of their existence, told artlessly, and with an unsuspected sublimity of pathos unknown to art.

'What shall I call you?' asked Emily, early in their confidential intercourse.

'Theodore,' replied the boy. 'That's my name.'

Commenting upon the oddity of the name to

her, the little girl repeated it several times to make sure of it.

With the cooler air of evening the strength of the boy's mother somewhat revived in her, and as she and Saloway walked up the twilight field in response to the dismissing bell which summoned them from their labours, the cobbler tried to elicit a few personal details from his new acquaintance; but beyond the fact of her name being Mrs. Carr it seemed impossible to go. Their homeward way lying in opposite directions, they had then to part.

The intenser heat of the following day found the scene in the pea-field but little altered. The glaring sun shone mercilessly down from its brazen sky upon the same ragged, half-naked company, amidst which was Benjamin Saloway tearing off the pods with silent assiduity, and not far away Theodore and Emily engaged in their lighter-hearted contest under the still tranquil eye of the problematic Mrs. Carr. The day wore on very much as the former one had done. But about mid-day, Emily, who paid increasing attention to Theodore's mother, saw her weep—the child distinctly saw the tears roll down her cheeks, glisten in the sun, and disappear. Only, with that precocious instinct of hers, she pretended not to see. Presently she whispered to her companion, 'Your mother's asleep.' The boy looked, and saw his mother comfortably reclining on the dry pease-straw. He just screened her head more effectually from the sun, and went back to work.

Through all the scorching afternoon Benjamin worked, the children worked, and the uneasy woman slept soundly. They would not even wake her to partake of food; Saloway, having his own little benevolent scheme for the time to come, noted her repose with peculiar satisfaction. He felt a renewed fervour for his life and work, such zest as he had deemed long since extinct in his adjustment to the world. His temporary unprecedented rate of earnings had no doubt affected him. Five shillings and tenpence had he carried home the day before, and to-day he saw every prospect of outstripping that. No wonder that he made light of brazen skies which had daunted stronger men than he. But at last the sun lowered, and Saloway trudged with what he feared was to be his last sack-load. The great crimson orb was sinking into the bank of dull purple haze which lined the north-west horizon behind the town, and the solemn hush which commemorates the close of another day was settling upon the land. Near at hand though it was, the ceaseless moan of the great human hive could not disturb the natural stillness, and, as Benjamin strode up the illumined field, his feet rustling in the dry haulm over which they trod, the quietude of the place overwhelmed him with the calm of other scenes. But this only served to confirm in him his increased vitality. Returning with his jingling wealth, he felt to be striding in the direction of a habitable world. Theodore was in the act of shouldering his full sack, with Emily's aid to balance it, amidst mirth in which the cobbler was able to take a part. He looked at the slumbering woman on the ground, and rubbed his hands. When the children came running down the field, he jocularly bade the boy awake his mother in preparation for the bell, whilst he took Emily away to gather up their own possessions.

As Benjamin leaned to the ground, the boy Theodore, who appeared silently and unexpectedly beside him, clutched the uncoated arm with a vehemence of grip which startled the cobbler.

He looked up, and with lips apart stared at the boy's features.

'What is the matter?'

'I can't wake her.'

'Can't wake her!'

'You come and try.'

Saloway turned pale as the twilight cloud overhead, and the perspiration rolled from his face as no sunbeams had been able to make it. He knew it all, but with a silent head-shake he accompanied the boy.

'Why, she be dead,' he said, raising up the woman's lifeless hand.

Benjamin hastened to summon the man in authority, just as the tones of his unmusical bell came upon the evening breeze to announce that the day was over, but his or other assistance was now vain. In the brazen sunlight the woman had slept her soul away.

CHAPTER III.

OUT OF THE DEEP.

THE public inquiry into that closing incident in the pea-field divulged one of the grim stories with which the impressible mind is only too familiar. Nothing was known of the woman, Mrs. Carr, beyond the fact, to which neighbours testified, that she had displayed signs of an extinct respectability amidst direst squalor. The immediate cause of death was of course starvation. She was presumably a widow ; at least, wore a wedding-ring, and the boy had never known a father. The paragraph was commented on at a hundred breakfast-tables, and the public conscience was appeased. But, as is customary in cases of the kind, the undergrowth of private benevolence was not wanting. Post-office orders for varying amounts poured in upon the coroner, and the starving orphan, announced to the world as Theodore Carr, was offered every possible kind of appropriate and inappropriate employment.

The matter was in the hands of the authorities, and they dealt with it in a humane and enlightened spirit. At the boy's own passionate entreaty all in-door apprenticeship was declined, for, to the cobbler's astonishment, Theodore protested his resolution to live with Benjamin Saloway and Emily. Whilst fully prepared to give due weight to so earnestly expressed a predilection, public duty necessitated a little investigation into this prospective guardian's moral and material condition. Benjamin's account of his own career, given, as may be supposed, with much reticence and even disguise, did not create a favourable impression. One too outspoken member hinted at the cobbler's possible trading on Carr. This aroused poor Saloway's anger, and at once decided his case.

'I have not asked the boy to come to me,'

cried Benjamin, with heightened colour, 'until he asked my little maid to let him go home with we I had no notion of such a thing. But being as the boy have so set his mind upon it I'll take him gladly and feed him well, but only on these terms, look you, that I touch ne'er a penny of his wages. Let his master keep they until the boy be old enough to have them for himself.'

The simple energy and sincerity of the man's speech and behaviour turned the general mind in his favour, and although a few questions in elementary theology were put to Emily to test Benjamin's general fitness and orthodoxy, the inquiry was practically at an eud. It was pointed out that if a man could bring up his child as Emily had evidently been brought up under such grossly unfavourable circumstances, it was ridiculous to pretend that he was unfitted for the custody of a boy eleven years old when the prospect was so obviously brightening. This statement was emphatically made by a pale-faced gentleman known to the company as a prosperous shoe-maker himself, and it was immediately whispered that Mr. Simpkinson had his eye on Saloway, which was as much as to say that they might put away the last of their scruples. This soon proved to be the case, for when the meeting broke up, this gentleman had a quarter of an hour's talk with the cobbler aside, which led to important changes in the latter's daily work and wages.

It had been decided, then, that Theodore Carr should take up his home with Saloway; that this latter should find, under the assistance and approval of the authority, a dwelling better suited to the fresh demands of his family; and that for employment the offer most advantageous to the boy would undoubtedly be that of Mr. Samuel Firkins, a well known timber-merchant on a large scale, the post in whose timber-yard was accordingly accepted on Theodore's behalf.

'A fortnight on Monday morning at nine o'clock I shall expect you to bring the boy to my office,' was Mr. Firkins' parting injunction to Saloway. 'He'll need that time to get to his feet again.'

Saloway was for a time overcome by his good

fortune.   So suddenly had the world, as he had known it, undergone a dazzling transformation that it was difficult for his clouded senses to associate the new appearance with any recognised habits of his own.   Not only was the incongruity passing strange; it was disquieting as it was wonderful.   It seemed a dragging out into the open of a shrinking soul whose only effort hitherto had been an avoidance of the light of day, a restless extinction of itself.

Familiarity with the change enabled the cobbler to surmount this morbid state, but not familiarity alone.   As all modifications of his existence hitherto had come through his own child Emily, so now was the development to be extended by Emily and the boy together.   Hardly with consciousness, Benjamin came to view the world through the eyes of these dependent children.   Wide fields were displayed to them of which Saloway in his time had never had so much as a glimpse, and although the man knew himself rigorously excluded from all participation in their wide prospect, it came to be a central purpose of his life that no rood of land should be with-held from them, no ray of sun obscured, through act or negligence of his.

Emily was forthwith sent to school, and great discussions arose out of her scholastic attainments in the Millington back street. Theodore, having been well trained, however indifferently fed, by his mother, was pronounced by the authorities sufficiently grounded in elementary knowledge for such path in life as he was likely to command : a verdict strenuously supported by Mr. Firkins, who entertained his own opinions as to the association of what we call education with a successful career in life.

Mr. Firkins himself was a man of some individuality. Some had expressed surprise at his having been drawn into the position of public benefactor, but to such he would not have deigned much light. Whatever his motive in seeking out the case, his personal examination of the boy seemed at once to confirm and intensify it. It was obvious that there was nothing sentimental about him. Of his private history, too, little was popularly known beyond the fact that he, like many in this industrial centre, had risen from submersion by dint of his own indefatigable energy. He was an unsociable man, unmarried, and indulged in but few of the ordinary diversions of his class. At this time he must have been nearing fifty years of age, and was of a harsh, unsympathetic exterior. His features, never regular, were somewhat marred by traces of small-pox, and his hair, bushy beard, and eyebrows once black, were now getting grizzled. Eyes were as clear and keen as ever. Altogether he was by no means the man to inspire confidence in timorous childhood, yet it is doubtful whether, in the same evil circumstance, the sensitive boy would have felt one whit the less keenly the vast bleak solitude of his universe, under hands which had lain in compassion on his wretchedness, and attempted to hide the thorns in his path under a haze of conventional maxims and benevolent misrepresentations.

What Carr did feel unmistakably was the strength of his employer, and this as a tonic was no doubt of peculiar value to him. When that Monday morning had duly come, Firkins himself initiated the boy into the mysteries of the timber-yard. He took him all round the extensive premises; displayed the vast accumulations of timber gathered from all corners of the globe; the cranes at work relieving the boats of their burdens; and finally, the interior of the saw-mills, whence issued those fearsome groans and shrieks, rising and falling in every tone of inexpressible torture and anguish, which had throughout their inspection frightened as well as mystified the nervous boy. In this department, it was pointed out to him, his work, would begin; Mr. Firkins remarking that twelve months sawdust was necessary for everybody entering the trade. In showing the timber-stacks he had already impressed upon the boy the necessity of geography, so that sawdust and geography came to be ludicrously intermingled in Theodore's brain, as of some mysterious efficacy in promoting that magical ‘ getting on ’ which everybody enforced so strenuously upon him.

From this commencement Theodore's advance was rapid; not so much from the purely mercantile point of view as from that of general development.   Commercial zeal was but one manifestation of the boy's many-sided character. His new domestic life was a revelation to him, and that old isolated companionship with his mother soon became but a dark cloud on the horizon, whereon the golden fringe of mutual devotion, it is true, for a long time lingered, but of which the main component was a dull chaos of tears and wretchedness.   The companionship of Emily appeared to Theodore now a perpetual holiday.   His old loneliness was at an end. Thus as Carr's sawdust work ministered to his active propensities, so did these domestic joys minister to his emotional and moral.   Soon, intellectual needs were added, which in their turn were fostered by the aid of some evening classes at a Mechanics' Institution not far from the street in which they lived.   It was soon obvious to all that this was a boy of uncommon spirit. Saloway especially made this discovery with pride, and through it he acquired an additional incentive to a more robust acceptance of life. On his own behalf he was no longer capable of ambition. That he might by daily labour continue to obtain his present modest livelihood was all that he desired; so infinitely more than anything he had ever hoped. That there was a different future before 'his boy' he never doubted, and he kept religiously before him the resolution to be nothing at all to the boy if not a direct assistance to his highest development.

Through these years Carr often spoke of the dazzling horizon before them all. He would return home at night from some triumphant. exercise of his intellectual faculties, all aglow with irrepressible enthusiasm before which all conceivable enterprise went down, and, as the cobbler pretended to read his newspaper, Emily, perhaps crouching on a stool, would fix her eyes in lustrous wonderment upon the energetic figure waving aside the narrow limits of the room enclosing it, and open her ears widely to the enchanting tales of the magic world beyond. Saloway saw much between the lines of his journal at those times.

One such evening Theodore and Emily were

alone, and they had been indulging in a more than ordinarily particular account of this glorious future. Then, as always, this blessed state was pitched amidst country scenes, and the youth had drawn with imaginative accuracy the very situation and appointments of the house in which they all should dwell. The necessary trees were planted, the flower-beds were in full bloom, and certain interior arrangements were about to be discussed, when an unwonted solemnity came over the girl's features, hitherto radiant with glee.

'It's too good to be true, Theodore,' said the child, now thirteen years old; but, seeing his ruffled brow, she added, quickly, 'At least, I mean, father and I shall not be there. I'm sure we can't be.'

'What rubbish, Emily! Do you think I shall live there if you won't come? There'll be no fun if we are not altogether. As if I should be rich if you and father won't share it.'

'But you will marry somebody,' said the little woman, sagely, 'and we couldn't all live in your house.'

The child had never hinted at such a possibility before, nor had the thought ever disturbed the shy boy in his calculations. Now Theodore blushed a little, although he averred angrily that he should never marry; not if it was to lead to their separation, at least not for a very long time.

'Besides,' he added, as a brilliant afterthought, seeing Emily continue pensive, 'why shouldn't I marry you when you are a woman? We are not real brother and sister, and they would let us. That would settle it.'

'Do you really think we might? . . . But, Theodore, I'm not good enough for you. You would have a real lady if you were rich, like Miss Wilson or Miss Jenkins.'

'No, I shouldn't,' asserted Carr, his shy disposition shrinking from such a situation. 'I shall marry you, Emily, if you will have me when you are old enough; and if you won't, we can all live together just the same. But here's father. Don't let him hear us talking about it.'

CHAPTER IV.

THE NEW.

NOT until Carr was nineteen did Mr. Firkins even partially withdraw him from the outside employment of the yard to take any recognized part in the internal machinery of the business, and it was the shrewd, independent exercise of the youth's commercial faculty that led to the modification of his work. In the course of his annual holiday that year, (Theodore was allowed a week of freedom every summer,) he came upon the sale of a bankrupt's stock of timber, and there and then bought it to very great advantage, getting by telegram his master's immediate confirmation of the transaction. Carr then quietly finished his holiday.

On his return Mr. Firkins had a characteristic interview with him,—thought he had better come into the office for a bit,—rated him for wasting his time on worthless studies,—'now had you known French and German, you might have undertaken some of the correspondence, and that idle scoundrel Jacques——'

'I can read and write French, sir.'

' Yes, *parlez-vous, comprenez-vous*, and so forth, I suppose; so can any fool that reads a newspaper. But you want a little more than that in here. You can't read that, for instance.'

Mr. Firkins thrust out the letter he had been handling, and Carr took it, reading it in English without hesitation. The dictated answer was as easily written in French.

'I didn't think you had so much sense,' was the master's comment, as he glanced at the sheet. 'Do you know anything else?'

' I am learning German and Spanish.'

' Oh, all right; you'll do for the present.'

Beyond a certain modification of the outer man, which more or less regular attendance in the office rendered necessary, Theodore made no change in his former course of consistent development. His emergence from boyhood had already brought the customary deliverance from angles, and it had been matter of common observation in the timber-yard that young Carr was getting very much a gentleman. A glance at him was enough to show that he was endowed with the instinct of polite aspirations, which there had been very little in his existence hitherto to foster. His natural thoughtfulness and reserve imparted to a graceful figure an air of dignity, and at this time, to a close observer, signs of a conscious culture and self-discipline might have been apparent. Benjamin Saloway, for instance, saw it clearly.

Under the guise of cynicism or indifference, Mr. Firkins also saw it all, and confessed secretly an unusual degree of satisfaction in the issue. He certainly did not feel tenderness for Carr; possibly it was merely selfish pride in him as a successful speculation. At any rate, as time advanced, the merchant became infected with a consuming need of exclusive possession of the youth, whence sprang an irritable jealousy, which resented the interposition of any other person. He overburdened Carr with work, for the sole purpose of keeping him at the office, and giving him less time to spend at home. He began to take him away on business—very soon to send him as his deputy on distant enterprises. Thus at last it came that Theodore was dispatched into Norway and Russia.

To one of Carr's intellectual vigour, this expedition to the Baltic was of the highest importance. The traveller was away a month, ostensibly investigating the state of the timber market, and actually doing it, but managing also to combine very much of a more liberal nature with this legitimate object of inquiry. Not content with the purely commercial element of Christiania and Drammen, from the inspection of timber-yards and mills, he passed to the contemplation of the pine-clad slopes that fed them. He crossed over to Riga; thence to St. Petersburg and Archangel. From every place he issued copious reports of his travels; one series for the eye of the practical, exacting master, another for devoted perusal by an obscure hearth in a back part of the town. These letters were from all points of view extremely interesting; to Saloway and Emily they were that, but they were very much more in addition. These two, in their stationary humility, were whirled on the ardent wings of the traveller's affection through all the scenes that he beheld, getting how much more than the mere vivid colouring that depicted them to the outward eye. The same note of personal love rang through the most brilliant words of description, and even the timorous cobbler was reassured. Emily had never as yet trembled, for she knew nothing of the nature of the abyss. She was now old enough to think with a blush of an incident of her childhood, and too old to remember the fear whence it had sprung. Theodore was now a world to her, and no state of existence was conceivable without him.

Carr returned, himself scarcely aware of the effect of this journey upon him, so full was he of the distracting details of all that he had seen. Even the dingy street did not immediately obtrude its disadvantages upon his enthusiastic senses, his gaze being fixed upon the radiant faces beyond. He had forbidden Emily and her father to meet him at the station, in view of his distaste for a greeting of that kind in the eyes of a crowd. So he walked in as though he had come from work; not owning even to himself that he had avoided a cab solely on account of a disinclination to speak to the driver the name of his street. As he crossed the threshold, he was conscious of a shock of incongruity and disappointment, but he smothered it in an embrace of Emily, who came into the passage to meet him.

The old frank buoyancy which Carr displayed throughout the evening permitted no critical consciousness amongst them. That he was more handsome than ever was thought enough for Emily, and with it she cried herself to sleep. Even Benjamin fell off to the soothing meditation that 'after all he was just the same.' But Theodore himself, when once the excitement of personal contact was over, found himself restless and depressed. As though to make up for those hours through which it had been defied, the critical spirit now rushed in for its revenge. The shock which Carr had resolutely crushed upon entering the house re-asserted itself, and diffused itself throughout the foundations of his being. All the joy with which he had looked forward to this return was annihilated by this pitiful infliction. All, all, he felt, was hideously, intolerably vulgar, and he felt a blush of shame at being an inmate of the dwelling.

When they all met in the morning, Carr was in his usual spirits, and no doubt designedly entered in that mood into his project. He jested about the narrowness of the rooms, the depressing nature of the outlook. He had never noticed it before; they must move. Emily entered readily enough into his humour, and before they parted after breakfast, the resolution was definitely formed.

'Why don't you talk about it, father?' asked the girl, when Theodore had left them. 'Don't you want to live in a nicer house?'

'I be'nt used to much, do you see, Emily. But don't fret about it, maidie; it be equally the same to I. Theodore must grow.'

Carr jocularly told Mr. Firkins of his decision, and was surprised at his manner of receiving it. The merchant hardly troubled to disguise his irritation. Seeing that the proposition involved a request for a substantial part of his savings, wherewith to furnish the new home, the youth not unnaturally mistook his master's attitude, and hastened to waive his own airy plans. Firkins answered it by flinging to him a cheque for a hundred pounds. Theodore would have spoken farther, but the other dismissed him in a rage. The next day, however, the elder was more affable.

'Why don't you live in lodgings?' asked the merchant. 'I thought you young men were all for freedom.'

'I'd rather live at home as long as I can,' said Carr.

Firkins turned away, and as he muttered something about 'queer tastes,' Theodore went out.

In a house, then, of twenty-five pounds a-year, with a bow-window, steps up to the door, and some square feet of begrimed grass

within iron railings was the Saloway family
established, and the click of the gate at any
hour of the evening was added to the trifles
having influence over Emily's heart-strings.
The internal harmony continued unbroken.
Perhaps Theodore was absent more than formerly, or when at home more frequently shut
up in the room which he had furnished himself
plainly for a study; but he was on the brink of
manhood, his intellectual activity was considerable, and his engagements consequently
more numerous.

It was, of course, his general development
that appeared in the privacy of home. To see
or hear him there, might have been to take him
for an intellectual aspirant exclusively, so little
of the commercial man was there clinging about
him. His discussions were instinctively intro-
duced from the imaginative standpoint. Although Carr had long since abandoned his
boyish handling of riches, it could be observed
that his attitude of mind habitually pre-supposed
wealth. For the last few years he had spent
all his week's holiday away from home; con-

sistently of late in tours comprising intellectual association. Birth and death places; castles and cathedrals; camps and battle-fields; had thus over a wide acre been visited by him, and always in intelligent connection with the facts which made them famous. All he saw he spoke about at home, so that his conversation was alike endless and entertaining, and thereby were Saloway and Emily enabled to make much general progress with him.

In his universal curiosity, Theodore's eyes, of course, did not overlook the present facts of his own circle. He had always shrunk from an investigation of his mother's history, but no doubt he pondered it not wholly without effect upon his emotional resources. With expanding intelligence, however, he viewed such points with broad interest and in connection with the social or political theories that appealed to him. Himself so essentially an outcome of the people, he had inevitably to pass through the more or less volcanic phases to which the self-confident imagination commonly succumbs; but the material smoothness of his path rendered the passage quick and easy. Oddly, too, his sympathies were essentially aristocratic; the ego being of a vigorous growth upon which he was rapidly borne into the optimistic ether wherein alone he could draw full breath. It was from that height that he regarded the darker world whence he had sprung; intelligently and sympathetically as becomes the serious patron.

He had talked frequently with Saloway of these problems as of others, pointing his remarks with direct personal inquiries, but always with disappointing results. So persistently had this been the case that it was some time now since Theodore had concluded that the cobbler had matters to hide. Benjamin would talk with manifest interest of problems in general, but once apply them to himself and he was dumb. He had confessed that he was country born; had spoken with energy on the subject of the agricultural labourer; but Carr had nothing else wherefrom to draw his inferences. As the young man grew older, this curiosity increased, and he showed a growing inclination for discussing rural problems with Saloway. Strange to say, the latter too made progress in communicativeness, or rather evinced indifference to sustaining his reserve.

The fact is that in these days the cobbler was conscious of a permanent alteration in his spirits. Although to all other eyes the prospect seemed of undiminished brilliance, he characteristically saw the clouds appear. The premonitory rumblings of certain incongruous elements in his existence kept him in a constant state of agitation. He had always said with pride that Theodore would get on, but only in these later years had he fully recognized how much this involved. Ever since that first expedition of Carr abroad, Benjamin had felt definite discomfort in the boy's presence, despite all the latter's affability and personal charm. The homely cobbler felt confronted by a superior world, from which everything that was instinctive in him impetuously shrank. Mere book-learning alone would never have vanquished him, had it been bound in plain leather boards. It was the development of Carr's binding that instituted the breach.

Nor did this exhaust the evils. Simple-minded as Saloway was, still was he super-sensitive on some points. Why should not Carr advance to any heights that his mind aspired to, and yet keep within genial hail of those below to whom, by his affections, he was bound? The experience is common, as even Saloway knew. But something persistently convinced him that this obvious path was not for them. Theodore's scrupulous temper had been amply revealed, and this, the cobbler felt, must preju-dice the boy's course. The father's eyes could now see his girl a woman, and herein lay the peril. The man could not escape a haunting con-viction that Theodore was not free. The very goodness of his heart would bind him, and urge him to a step which his interests, possibly his passions, would not demand. In this light did Saloway distort all kinds of innocent displays. If Carr were absent or shut up for half-an-hour more than was his wont, the youth was design-edly avoiding Emily; if she were playfully talkative with Carr, then was she forcing her-self upon his affections.

It was these morbid fancies that induced Saloway's indifference to old secrets of his own. Perhaps some vague reflection hinted that a full revelation of his past ignominy would simplify the situation by damping Carr's affection and affording him an outlet for escape. Thus it came that one evening, in discussing country affairs, the name Winwold issued boldly from the cobbler's lips, and in such connection as to leave no room for doubt in one of Theodore's acuteness. Thinking it a slip, incident to momentary excitement, Carr let it pass without comment; but the name was on his mind, and the next day he looked out the place. One night, a day or two after this, Carr, coming in late, found Benjamin alone reading. In taking his chair the former remarked that the next week he was to have his holiday, and Saloway, as was usual, asked him where he was going.

'To Gloucester first, and then into South Wales.'

'Gloucester,' muttered the cobbler, scarcely knowing that he fixed his eyes wide upon the other's face.

Theodore adroitly launched into an account of the various other places he had thought of, when unexpectedly Saloway clutched his arm.

'Go to Winwold,' said he, almost in a whisper. 'I'd like you to see it, and I'd like to hear you talk about it, that I would, for I'll never go there myself again, never!'

Carr took up the suggestion good-humouredly, and inquired the way and all about the place. Then, for the first time through a long, dark series of years, the exile voluntarily recalled the scenes of his youth. He confessed that he was born there, and had lived there till twenty-five; but upon the subject of his departure he preserved a rigid silence. As he approached the chasm his courage forsook him, and, his agitation becoming extreme, they very soon parted for the night.

During the next few days Benjamin was more composed, and he spoke in a calmer spirit of the scenes that Theodore was to see. But nothing personal was again disclosed. Only when Carr was leaving for the station the cobbler whispered to him,

'Breathe ne'er a word about I; it'll bring no credit to you.'

When he had taken a few steps along the pavement, Theodore turned to wave his hand once more to those whom he knew would watch him to the farthest limit, and he saw Saloway running hatless towards him. Carr stopped.

'Go in by the Upton Quarr,' said the cobbler, and fled; for his eyes were full.

CHAPTER V.

A VISION.

IT was always a strange sensation to Carr this first awakening in the dawn which opened upon his week of annual holiday. It generally occurred in the same kind of little inn bed-room, to the same musty breath of bed-post and hangings, to the same homely talk of the pigeons on the roof, and the same clatter of the pump-handle in the yard. These were now an inseparable part of the impression, and Theodore loved them all, and rose to a high pitch of enthusiasm under their subtle influence.

So it was when he opened his eyes in the guest's best bed-room at the 'Frog Mill Inn,' in the village of Winwold. He always awoke early at such times, and for long he lay regarding the faded hangings suspended from the canopy of his bed, and trying to disentangle the old pattern from the mists and cobwebs which years had woven about it. The spirit and very features of Benjamin Saloway seemed involved therein, in a most unaccouutable manner; indeed one of the most noticeable impressions upon Theodore since he entered the parish by the Upton Quarry on the previous day had been the subtle interweaving of the cobbler's personality with everything about the place. He seemed as inevitable a product of this slumbering country as the stolid cows or shaggy horses that still fed upon it.

In au exalted condition Carr left his bed, just as the sun's rays first printed the inner wall with the pattern of the lattice window. He hummed, whistled, and sang snatches of melody as he hastily dressed, then he went forth. Outside, everything united to further his buoyant mood. The sounds and fragrance of the June air swept in at every pore; the artist thrush, the pensive blackbird soliloquizing ethic truth, and the heavenly lark, seemed, through the magic of the morning sun, to meet and combine in the soul of Theodore Carr. In him the eternal problem was solved, and he waded the fields an immortal.

In this exuberant state he met a middle-aged countryman, with whom he stopped to speak. Directly the man's tongue had spoken, the parental Saloway appeared with almost ludicrous distinctness.

'Did you ever hear of Benjamin Saloway?' asked Carr, after the general remarks.

The man eyed him and shook his head.

'Dead long since, I count.'

'You knew him, then?'

'Ay, ay, I knew he well. But mebbe you know 'un an' all, sir?'

'Yes, some years ago I did. He was very kind to me when I was a boy.'

'That he 'ud,' said the countryman, whose features displayed uncommon interest. 'And be he alive then, after all?'

'I believe he is, and getting on well.'

'Well, well, I'd never ha' thought that, however.'

' Why not ?'

' Oh, 'em crippled him cruel when 'em sent him off to Glorster. A were but a shadow of a man when a came back.'

' Why, what was it all about ?'

'A long tale, sir, and a dark one, as I may say to you,' replied the man, looking cautiously around him. 'It was along o' the squire sure enough,' he added, in an undertone. 'Benjamin Saloway said to I in the Upton Quarr yonder, the very day as a left Win'ol, and that were twenty-two years past on the Tuesday afore Upton Wake, —for that was the very day as a was drove from this parish, having come from Gloucester gaol but the day before—quite a young man a was, but something out of the common, I do believe, and always given to learning, and a was like one sacrificed, as you may say. What for ? . . . Poaching was the item, so 'em said, do you see ? . . . But to cut a long story short, sir, Ben stood there in the quarr, his eyes set as solid as a owl on the cider mill, and a spoke quite solemn. " Thomas Warrilow," a said, " I be a-going from Win'ol; druv out like a rat from a thrashing rick, and I'll never come back, look 'e. But you'll see it, and when you be an old man ou the parish you'll mind the words of a despert man," just like that. "If there be a God in that blue heaven, as Scriptur do plainly tell us there be,"—that's what a said, sir, for Benjamin never professed the principles of athaism, very far from it, for all the squire said, although a many did at that time o' day, more's the pity,— "If there be a God in that blue heaven, as Scriptur do plainly tell us there be, a'll visit the iniquity o' the fathers upon the children unto the third and fourth generation, and the family o' Blakenhurst 'ull be drove from the acres as they have withheld from the cry of the poor, just as I be a-driven out o' my home at this minute." Those were his very words, sir, and I'll never forget 'em, never.'

'I should think not,' said Carr, upon whom the picturesque narrative exercised a singularly thrilling effect. 'But what led the squire to drive him out, since you say poaching was only a pretence?'

''Lotments was the real concern. The squire

got a notion that poor Ben was one of these revolutionaries, as he called 'em; them as burn ricks and all manner; but a wasn't. Oh, dear, no. A wanted to get land for the like of we, and a went to ask for it, that was all. But as I may say to you, sir, Squire Blakenhurst can't abide a poor man nohow, never could from a boy.'

'Can't he?' said Theodore, absently; and thrusting half-a-crown into the man's hand continued his walk onwards.

The brief conversation had afforded all he was in need of, and it threw into a new and dramatic light many of the cobbler's opinions upon the problems of rural life. Carr pondered them once again as he made his way back to the village inn.

The effect of the discovery, however, soon passed, in the face of so much that was exhilarating all around him. The weather remained exquisite, and Carr found the idyllic locality to inspire him with a peculiarly strong imaginative fervour. For long days he wandered over the uplands where the sheep and lambs nibbled, startling the hawks in old-world quarries, from which nature had long since smoothed all traces of the tools of man. He crouched in the sombre quietude of larch groves to hear the wood-pigeon's tale, or with hand upon the motionless bark to watch the swaying crests of the young trees up in the sun. He threaded the green labyrinth upon the slopes of fragrant gorse, playing without restraint those games of hide and seek with the rabbits of which his own childhood had been cheated. Amidst these sunny scenes, in this state of imaginative ex-altation, one day he became suddenly aware that he was alone; that he knew the desire to communicate his enthusiasm to a sympathetic ear. It is not at all likely that a youth of Theodore Carr's marked sensibility had reached the age of twenty-three without some haunting suspicion of this before, but it had certainly never been so definitely pronounced. He began to seek the woods instead of the open hill-tops, and in every glade lurked ethereal figures which he wished to overtake, but which flitted on with tender beckoning glances. At length, in the glow of sunset, one he captured. As he emerged from a wood, in front of three tall pine-trees whose trunks and branches had become pillars of rosy granite in the gorgeous light, in fancy he resolutely caught her hand, and, turning the averted face to his own eager gaze, recognized the familiar features of his companion Emily.

A tremulous satisfaction pervaded Carr upon this discovery. That evening he absented himself from the homely gossip in the parlour of the 'Frog Mill' that he might contemplate the revelation beneath the few faint stars of the summer sky. By a flash of apprehension many incidents in their home-life acquired new light to him. He dwelt upon them eagerly and with irresistible conviction. What he had always passed as the mere kindliness of domestic affection he now saw to be something more. Could he now doubt that Emily loved him, as he would willingly confess that he loved Emily?

On the following day, whilst pursuing the ardent thoughts which this admission gave rise to, Theodore came to a spot which greatly delighted him. It was one of those deserted quarries which he discovered occasionally; one which, lying silent in the high morning sun, looked peculiarly inviting to one in his transcendent mood. As Carr entered it by the disused and overgrown cart-track to stand in the quietude of the little amphitheatre, at the top of which against a clear sky he saw the young corn waving, a sense of solemnity crept over him. He stood to watch the rabbits scamper home to their shelter in the stony bank, and the one hare bound up the acclivity and clear the rim into the corn. Then he went to a solitary block of rough unhewn stone which had been left in the open centre, lichened and blackened by long exposure, and there sat down.

First of all, his botanical eye examined all the kindly weeds which had aided the grass to clothe the stony bareness which man had left; but, his eye travelling to the brilliantly flecked sky which over-arched his little basin, emotional thoughts were not long excluded. In the quiet sun he sat and reflected, breaking the silence sometimes by a sharp stroke of his stick upon a stone, but otherwise only hearing the light breeze rustling the blades of corn, the skylark's song, or a rook which croaked as it sailed lazily above him. He thought that his holiday was ending, and with the thought his joy was less. This was not customary with him. He must return—to what? To Emily, certainly; but was it not *here* that he had found Emily? Was it not these sunlit woods and fields that her soul inhabited, and by no means those hard blank cells where her daily life was passed? Never before had the world of man appeared other than attractive to the youth. Now he shrank from it; longed to snatch from its poisonous fangs everything he loved, and hide for ever in this heavenly seclusion.

It was from such thoughts as these that a resonant laugh aroused him. So incongruous was it that Carr leaped up. The sound was repeated,—a musical and sparkling laugh as of some gladsome spirit of the air. The man stared this way and that, expecting some apparition at once to follow; but he stared in vain. The enclosing sides of the quarry were alone around him ; the silent sky alone above. So Theodore again sat down.

Scarcely was he seated, when there was a sound behind, and turning he saw the light figure of a girl swiftly descending the steep slope which the hare had climbed. Carr rose to his feet and waited. About two yards from him the figure halted, and eyed him imperiously. The bashful youth was perplexed, so striking was his opponent in herself and in the singular attitude she adopted.

' Why do you intrude here?' she asked, in queenly accents. ' This spot is mine.'

So completely was Theodore fascinated by the romantic incident that in his confusion he did not even mutter an apology. With slight increase of colour over his smooth features, he kept his eyes fixed upon the beautiful girl. That she was quite young was apparent, for her frock was above her feet and her luxuriant hair was flung about her head in exquisite disorder. Her complexion was clear and beautiful, the colour of it enriched by her recent exercise. But she was tall, and the free play

of her loose muslin frock, with a coloured sash
at the waist, showed every girlish grace of form
and movement. Then the sweet refinement of
her tongue, even in what Carr instinctively felt
to be affected anger, thrilled him to the core.
The man continued dumb.

'Speak,' she said, as though construing his
confusion and accustomed to such display
before her.

'I saw that the spot was beautiful, but I did
not know it to be yours,' said Carr, smiling as
the advantage of his years became clear to him.
His voice and his reply surprised her, as perhaps his whole mien, now that she could see it
near.

'It is all mine; every stone, every flower, and
every blade of grass that is in it, and I punish
those that dare to enter.'

'I am now willing to undergo any punishment,' said Theodore, gallantly, willing to sustain her humour, if only it might prolong his
glimpse of such a creature, and the sound of
such a voice. 'Name it.'

'You do not live in this parish,' was the inconsequent reply.

'I do not, or perhaps I should have known your law and have respected it.'

'For that word I forgive you, but I do not think I ought, for you have even plucked my flowers.' Her eye had just caught sight of the few specimens which Carr had laid upon the stone whereon he sat.

'They were gathered before I entered here.'

'Are you a herbalist, or a botanist?' asked the girl.

'The latter I suppose you would call me. But I gather flowers for the same reason that you possess them.'

'What reason is that, may I ask?'

'Because I love them.'

'How do you know that I love my flowers?'

'You must.'

The girl seemed instinctively to foresee the compliment, and with supreme composure to waive it. She turned as though to leave.

'Well, I will allow you to sit here,' she said, scarce able to repress her smile as she became conscious of her lapse. ' *You* will not desecrate the place.'

Carr made a courtly obeisance.

'May I beg a single flower in remembrance of my trespass, and to confirm my pardon ?'

' Yes, you may have one.'

' From the hands of the queen of the garden, I meant,' he pleaded.

Theodore's frame quivered at his boldness, for habitually he was no adept in such tender pleasantries, and whatever her age, the aspiring clerk could not but perceive the social extraction of the divine phantom. The queen seemed not to hear him ; but then she leaned to the ground and plucked a large moon-daisy, (as the wild marguerites there were called,) and refaced Carr. The beautiful features were under supreme command this time, and with really very much of queenly grace and dignity, the strange maiden bestowed her favour upon Theodore, who as no unworthy courtier received it. Then the vision passed.

Carr was left in a state of higher commotion than his years and experience warranted. Acting upon an already over-heated fancy, the exploit, which he could see to have been but a momentary whim of an intrepid, imaginative girl, took him at a disadvantage, and made a deeper impression upon him than any outcome of superabundant idleness justified. All else was driven from his mind, and he sat with his eyes to the ground, recalling every minutest detail of the exquisite apparition. Every spark of the critical faculty was for the nonce extinguished in him ; he only gazed to recover, recovered to adore. It was as though another higher embodiment of all his recent sunlit abstractions had been revealed to him, eclipsing all behind. It almost lost touch with a material world, and became a dazzling meteor, traversing the spheres.

At the inn later, in a more sober mood, he talked with the landlady, and had little difficulty in identifying his apparition as a creature of flesh and blood, familiar to her world as Miss Laura Blakenhurst, daughter of the middle-aged squire who reigned in Winwold, and upon the fact Theodore sagely reflected.

CHAPTER VI.

THE GODS OF WINWOLD.

WINWOLD, as other most secluded of rural places. had altered with the times. The mixture of genuine calm and sullen self-containment which characterised its pre-journalistic days had, since the time of Saloway, been gradually but surely invaded by the stealthy pace of disintegrating forces. Its spectacular charm was unimpaired; the sun still illumining the same moss-grown roofs in the morning, and capping with a crown of gold the same tall elms in the evening, as it had done for generations past. The owls hallooed, the wood-peckers laughed, and the jays cursed, as heartily as ever over the swelling downs. The human element alone could be accused of having forfeited its native dignity by lapse of time, of having dwindled to the ignoble limits of the day's unrest, until now the village had become that normal and inevitable group of detached, indifferent, nay, bitterly antagonistic units which sages have pronounced to be the extinction of all strength. Roughly the population could be divided into three classes. Those who at the plough, upon the ale-bench, and in other convenient places, railed vernacularly against the whole nature of established things ; those who, copying the upper, distrusting the lower classes, trembled for their modest investments, and over the social tea-cup speculated upon the tragic destiny of a world with which they were once familiar ; and those finally who of more or less cosmopolitan propensities cared no whit for any of these things.

Contemporaneous as this chanced to be with the reign of Mr. Geoffrey Blakenhurst, it were puerile to associate its course with him personally in face of the universal development of his time. That the squire laid no claim to enlightenment we know, but possibly in such obscurity

he was not alone. He sprang from such family
as we have agreed to call ancient and honour-
able. Knights and baronets had been freely
numbered amongst his ancestors in the old fight-
ing days, and their fearsome deeds were duly
chronicled in the proper pages. The generations
of recent centuries had been content to remain
landed esquires merely. Yet were the Blaken-
hursts of Winwold, through their Geoffreys,
Rolands and Reginalds of post-restoration days,
of some imperial reputation beyond the leafy
confines of their proprietary county. The
Reginald Blakenhurst who contested the reign
of Marlborough with such signal consequences
to himself was lord of this manor of Winwold.
Geoffrey, a recognized antagonist of George
Fox, was a son of the same house, whilst Mr.
Lionel Blakenhurst who, within the memory of
some living, died of an apoplectic fit in his place
in the House of Commons whilst energetical-
ly opposing his last breath to the Reform Bill
of '32, was this phantom Laura's own grand-
father, the parent of the lord in whose name the
chief-rents of the Winwold Manor ran at the

time when Theodore Carr now first beheld it.

Degenerate as in some respects he would legitimately have been considered, it had been reserved for this nineteenth century representative of the race to confront issues of striking novelty in the family annals, for which all the martial and political prowess of his ancestors could not supply a precedent; this novelty being presented in the form of intellect, and under the fascinating aspect of his daughter Laura.

The squire's family consisted of a son and heir, Vivian by name; a daughter Pauline, at this time meditating marriage; another son Walter; and finally Laura. The last from her birth had been regarded as the exception to the family, a brilliant singularity where all was by rule. Rather oddly, it was thought, her engaging unexpectedness could to nobody make more engrossing appeal than to her matter-of-fact father. It was more or less jocularly reported that the tragic fate of the Reform Bill antagonist had extinguished promising talents in his son, (although but a schoolboy of sixteen at the time,) and with them

all shade of extraparochial ambition. It was an
undoubted fact that Mr. Geoffrey Blakenhurst
had abandoned himself to a strictly domestic,
or at any rate manorial career.

Such affections, then, as the lord of Winwold
might have at his disposal would be presumably
bestowed upon his immediate family or his
estate; but as nobody ever heard him speak of
his tenantry save by way of unreserved vilification
and disgust, and as no member of his family except Laura had ever been aware of his most
superficial regard, it is to be presumed that yet
a further limitation was put upon his affections,
and that it was Laura herself who monopolized
the whole of what was known to her father as
love. It was never doubted but that this
devotion was fully reciprocated by the brilliant
object of it. A word from the squire could
summon the high-spirited child from the
most engrossing diversion; and, still later, no
demand was too exacting for the patience of the
girl. She it was who read him the local
Journal, *The Field*, and what he required of *The
Times*; and she it was who slipped away when his

faculties had duly succumbed to the strain thus put upon them. The parent, on his part, never tired of superintending what he considered the main part of his favourite's education,—what related, that is, to the stable, the kennel, and the field. In trivialities, the assistance of a more conventional governess was not forbidden, and thus it was that Laura had advanced robustly to the years of early maidenhood.

As fate would have it, though, this governess whom the squire deemed so insignificant an adjunct of his establishment, was not the conventional nonentity that the gentleman's estimate would have led one to expect. Her name was Miss Birdwell, and under a placid affability and unconcern there lurked an unusually speculative and imaginative temperament. By inevitable instinct the child Laura had early seen her way to the depths of this individuality, and in a situation not too abundantly agreeable the intelligent pupil was not a companion to be despised. Through this intimacy, Laura first found guidance and systematic development in her unbounded youthful curiosity. The first obvious outcome of it was merely a heightening of her piquant characteristics, and a corresponding increase of admiration in her father who observed it. He could never sufficiently repeat her witty or cynical remarks, and, so scant is our average logic, he could not so much as suspect their germ of practical antagonism to his own acquiescent modes. This, however, Laura very early did suspect, and it imposed the first strain of self-consciousness upon her. There followed the inevitable dissimulation and reserve under guise of boisterous frankness. Laura posed before her father; acted a conscious part, such as she knew to be expected of her, solely to humour him, to adjust herself to what she adjudged his ignoble level. Her high spirits resented such tactics in the beginning, and hot arguments were held with Miss Birdwell in favour of establishing intellectual confidence with the squire, but the precocious girl was speedily convinced of her quixotic wish.

What heightened the difficulty was that it was in no creed of merely flippant cynicism that Laura had been confirmed by her intimacy with the enthusiastic governess. This lady was of obscure extraction, whom sheer intellectual stress had thrust unaided above the current, and, as was not unnatural to one in such independent case, she found all her strength in purely elementary forces. Thus Thomas Carlyle was her prophet, and the *Latter Day Pamphlets*, for chief, her confession of faith: a loud note of incongruity, it may be presumed, in the house of the lord of Winwold. If the sage's sartorial semblances, unveracities, and chimeras dire found anywhere their exemplification in the world of fact, it was surely here in the squirearchical establishment of an upland corner of the county of Gloucester. This uncompromising creed exercised its fascinations over the warm-hearted Laura, despite her more strictly dramatic sympathies, with at length its logical practical issues. There was so much of the Blakenhurst instinct in her as to preclude wholly the ignoble refuge of merely passive theory, and, as may be surmised, her father's territories offered a peculiarly favourable field for energetic practice. Hence still further developments in the tangles of a double life, for the squire's angry antagonism to all contemporary problems and requirements was familiar to all. If such matter were so much as broached in his hearing, he never failed to meet it with the now locally proverbial boast of his manner of dealing with the revolutionary cobbler, Benjamin Saloway, in his younger days. With justifiable pride and assurance, the squire truly emphasized the fact that nobody had ventured to repeat the experiment since that time.

Such then was the week-day reality of the apparition which had at a critical moment and in a fit of frolic flitted across Theodore Carr's path. General inquiry gave him the bare family facts, which he wove in characteristic fashion about the creation of his own. But when he visited the quarry the next morning (the opening of his last free day), his brain was calmer, his vision more clear. That this late-seen spirit of the skies should have (as all had told him) as ' kind a heart as any in the country,' he could well believe, but the discovery of her earthly lineage was at first disquieting. Generous loyalty to Saloway had awakened instinctive indignation against the tyrannical squire, and it required some subtle reconciliation to be able to associate in one mind these opposing elements.

In approaching this, we must bear in mind that the sudden and irresistible effect of the vision upon Carr was not wholly the result of mere youthful sentiment. It was in reality as much an intellectual as an emotional effect, although under the circumstances the latter forces seemed naturally to be supreme. For some years the youth's self-culture had been a conscious design and aspiration, and at such age the crowning height must involve something of the feminine. This highly-bred and beautiful girl, having appeared to him so strangely at a moment of such exceptional susceptibility, had by her figure, mien, tone, and behaviour simply presented to his waking eye the incarnation of his spiritual idea. She embodied the ideal of life which had actuated all his more recent endeavour, or seemed to him to embody it. She seemed to present to him all that his soul and

brain demanded for its loftiest existence, which
presumably the homely virtues of Emily did
not, else would not these latter have withstood
the contrast?

Carr had a dim perception of this as he sat
again on the stone with his intellectual task to
perform. It could not accord with his philosophy to accept the daughter as the perfection
of all human development, and the father as the
type of its most brutal form. Some middle
course was imperative in a cause where he was
conscious of conflicting instincts. Saloway, who
was a father to him, had been barbarously
wronged; the fact clearly was not to be con-
troverted. Without suspecting casuistry, Theodore penetrated to the depths of that ancient
difference, and came out triumphant. His own
position, he deemed, gave him exceptional capabilities for seeing into this matter,—hanging
between the two worlds as he always considered himself. From such position nothing had
so strongly assailed him as the utter incompatibility between the upper and the nether. In
the case in hand, had not both sides been in the

wrong through sheer stress of this incompatibility? The fanatical sincerity of the cobbler, coupled no doubt with an utter want of judgment in his method, had jarred upon the refined perceptions of the squire, and led him into a harsh misconstruction of his suppliant. Carr saw no egoism in such arbitration. Instinct was still philosophy with him. The consequence was that his affection for the sufferer was unimpaired, and his vision of ideal grace suffered no blur from the base clouds of kinship.

But Theodore was not without a sense of the vital significance of the change which had come over him. He was quite aware that his recent transfiguration of the purely personal in Emily was a dangerous illusion, in which for him would have lain eclipse and general disablement. Love, such as he had recently admitted for Emily, of course meant marriage, and in the light of all his highest aims what did he expect from marriage? Could Emily bring all this to him? . . . If she could not . . . ?

His invocation of the vision was without avail. Only a single magpie flew out of the quarry before him as he left it, and chattered something which he did not understand. In the evening of that day he returned to Millington.

CHAPTER VII.

WHERE THE ROAD DIVIDES.

SALOWAY quivered in every fibre as he listened to Theodore's graphic reproductions of the scenes amidst which both of them had spent the past week. The enthusiasm and unconscious artistic skill with which Carr revealed all the subtle influences of Benjamin's early and only home disquieted the latter by arousing associations which the exile preferred to keep deeply hidden in his heart.

'And the field at the boundary, Theodore, anear the beeches—what be the crop this turn ?'

'Mostly poppies, with some sort of grain intermingled,' was the facetious answer.

' Well, well, 'twere ever so. It needed a deal
of hoving did that land, and never got it—
never in Master Honyatt's time, however. Who
have the place now? Not the old man . . . ?
Can't, o' course, for a was over seventy when—
years ago. Dead by now, sure to.'

Upon these points Theodore could give no
information, but they confronted him at every
turn in the conversation, and as they afforded
opportunities of indulging his playful humour
they did no disservice. Emily took little part
in the talk, but she listened with intense interest, and, as Carr poured forth his glowing
words, he became uneasily conscious from time
to time of the girl's ardent eyes fixed upon him.
But he would turn to sustain them with every
appearance of genial unconcern. That night,
however, Theodore could not sleep.

He returned to his daily work with a sense of
wearisome disgust which was wholly new to
him. The employment had become paltry and
ignoble in his eyes, and therefrom sprang fits
of abstraction in him who had been all vigorous
activity before. If he were writing a letter, he

would pause with the pen-handle to his lips and gaze at the timber stacks outside, until each rigid beam became supple and graceful, wafting to him the soft whispers of leaves long since mouldered beyond a rustle. The arid world about him dissolved into a rich and fragrant one, wherein the wings of imagination might spread themselves and soar into the light of heaven. He was recalled to the sordid facts of life with a pang, and could face them only with supremest effort. Life lay upon him as an intolerable burden, instead of being an unconscious inspiration of buoyant good as heretofore. He suspected himself to be one hopelessly debarred from light.

Such an unusual sensation inevitably affected his outward bearing. His numerous interests waned; scenes wherein he had displayed unbounded energy knew him no more. He trudged wearily along the streets from his dwelling to his work, from his work to his gloomy dwelling again, with scarcely a glance around him. Nobody detected the change so readily as his two domestic intimates, but they were reticent, towards him and towards each other. The gloom of Theodore settled upon the household, as though no sun but his could enter it. Saloway, drawing his own conclusions, felt his home a place of torture, and began to spend all his spare time in a public reading-room, in the vain pursuit of distraction outside himself. Carr passed his time alone in his room, nobody knew how. Emily sat with her needle, solitary.

One night, as she sat so, Theodore came from his room impetuously. He was going out, but, seeing the girl dejected there, he found it impossible to pass her. He went in and stood before her chair. She, seizing the opportunity, looked up at him.

'You are tired, Theodore; you work too hard.'

Carr laughed in a hollow, unpleasant manner.

'Work, Emily! I have not worked since I returned from Winwold. It is just because I am unable to work that I have made such a fool of myself. For some time I have felt that I should die if I did not go to live in the fields. I have thought of the most frantic schemes, even to becoming an agricultural labourer!'

Again the laugh grated harshly on Emily, and she looked down silently.

'But no, no,' cried Theodore, 'we must be rich first—and then!'

There was a momentary flash of his old determination, and Emily's eyes were instantly upon him.

'Rich—we must be rich. There can be no real happiness without it; no advance, no beauty in life. What is life if we don't attain to the very highest that life can give? Only with wealth can we attain it. All culture of the human soul springs from wealth, as all squalor and degradation from poverty. We have been cursed in our birth, Emily, but we have weapons, and we can fight. We will carve our way to it. I begin to see the light again, and I shall work. Work, work, night and day, to be rich. My riches shall buy me light; shall buy us all light; if not, we will heave them into the sea. Fear for me no longer.'

It was thus that Carr announced the truce

which he had come to, and, however her religion regarded it, Emily accepted the terms gladly and silently. Any change upon recent days was acceptable. Had there not been good religious rich men? And would not Theodore Carr be another of them? She accepted the sincere conviction that the breeze had sprung up. In a day or two Saloway himself discerned the change, and soon discovered the source of it, from which he gathered scant comfort. The cobbler could not but feel that high mysteries were weaving about his life, and in the timidity of his nature he distrusted them. Theodore seemed to have regained the whole of his external energy and most of his former health; but there was a difference in his domestic aspect. He was kind, inordinately kind,—unnecessarily generous; but everybody felt that he was no more a boy. There were none of the old heedless confidences, none of the enthusiastic talk. If he brought home a new book or engraving, it was put silently aside instead of being displayed jubilantly to Emily, and its attractions pointed out. Needless reticences sprang up amongst them which inevitably sapped all common life. Saloway grew dumb. Theodore alone seemed to be insensible to the evil effects of the change. He toiled still and flourished. In all personal appointments he was progressive, without affectation or bad taste. He had a drawer at a toilet club, and bills with his tailor were increasing. Yet he simply looked a gentleman, as anybody with the requisite instinct is permitted to do in our day.

'He ben't one of we,' had long been poor Saloway's melancholy conclusion, and in these days it was reiterated frequently.

With Mr. Firkins Carr continued in increasing favour,—evidenced by excessive multiplication of his responsibilities without any proportionate increase in his pay. But of this Carr directly thought little. The tendency of things he considered to be now obvious, and he was content to be patient. His wages were far in advance of his personal wants, and for petty hoarding he had no faculty.

Despite all this individual adjustment, Carr was

constantly aware of one central difficulty which he had not yet touched. To his own development he could not be blind, and he admitted it to surpass his boldest expectations. The development of Saloway and Emily was by no means so inevitable a matter. Nobody had a truer estimate of personal worth than Theodore, or a more scrupulous sense of generous honour, hence had all Mr. Firkins's insidious attempts to decoy him from his plebeian atmosphere been of no avail. That such atmosphere was intolerably oppressive to the youth we know, but it was only through personal endeavour, not ignoble flight, that he looked for a remedy. He would not escape from, but he would transform the atmosphere which was so repugnant to him.

A timely increase of wages enabled him at length to assail the evil in its citadel, and he opened fire immediately. His tactics inevitably took a magnanimous complexion. In telling Saloway of his advance, Theodore boldly submitted his proposition, which was simply this: Benjamin was to cease entirely his labours; a house was to be found at a reasonable distance from the town, with a garden and perhaps additional land whereon the cobbler could find congenial work and satisfy his conscience by raising produce for the market; all the expenses of the establishment were to be upon the disinterested proposer, who could pass to and fro for business purposes. As Carr enlarged with enthusiasm upon the delights and manifest advantages of his proposal, Emily looked radiantly upon him, her faith in a moment restored, and her love for Theodore inconsiderately exhibited. Saloway received it more calmly, as befitted his maturer years.

'It be good of you, Theodore; uncommon good,' he said, deliberately; 'but that, of course, you have ever been. However, it ben't a thing to decide all of a minute. We'll think about it a bit.'

Carr acquiesced, and beyond that they did not go that night.

Although Saloway was thus able to temporize, the suggestion came to him as a final blow, so exactly did it coincide with sundry communings of his own at the time. He had

long since concluded that the domestic situation
was not to be maintained; this gave him the
opening that he had needed.

In the morning, as Carr set off to work, the
cobbler accompanied him; he generally went
some time before. Theodore felt the significance,
so he assumed an unusually jocular air.

'You are going to agree?' he said, before they
had gone many paces.

'Not entirely, Theodore,' was the measured
reply. 'I could never give up my work and become little more than a log on the earth, for I
be too old to begin a new trade, do you see,
and I doubt I ben't strong enough for digging.
But look 'e, boy, I don't mean as that shall stand
in the way of *you*. There be a vast odds between your life and mine, thank God as I have
lived to see it. All birds have to leave the nest
at some time, o' course, and the time have come
for you to leave yours, I count. You'll be a
great man, but that don't say as you'll ever forget we, very far from it, I know. But you must
go, Theodore. If I have ever done any small
good to you, you mustn't make me undo it now

at last.   You'll come and see me sometimes—'

'Do you think I shall ever do this?' interposed Carr, vehemently.

'Not only shall, but must, my boy.   It be for *I* as you must do it.   I've seen it a-coming.   I be a-hindering you, Theodore, a-hindering you, and I wunt do it, not nohow.'

The man shook with the vehemence of his conviction.

'If you love me ever such a bit you must go. Do you think as I can live on and see you hindered by the like o' me?   I'll take money from 'e—plenty—I'll take anything as you like to give; but, Theodore, you must go——'

'No, father, I shall not go.   Leave you, leave Emily, just because—bah, I couldn't!   Let us stay where we are and forget all about it.'

'Not when we have got our foot so far,' said Benjamin, with undiminished fervour.   'I've wanted to say it to you, times, but I couldn't. Now it be said, I'll not unsay it, never.   It be for your good, Theodore, and that be the conclusion of the matter.'

'Well, well, we'll talk about it again,' said Carr, in a kindly tone, and with an affectionate nod went off in another direction.

Carr was told that the master had been clamouring for him, so he went forthwith to the presence.

'What are you late for?' roared Mr. Firkins, when he saw the youth.

'I was detained——'

The merchant interrupted him with an imprecation, and thrust a letter into his hand.

'You must go down at once and see to this. If you miss the ten o'clock, you'll hear about it.'

The communication had reference to some timber shipped to Hull.

'Look here,'—Carr was standing in the doorway,—'you'd better go on to Newcastle when you're there, and see Davidson.'

'Very good, sir;' and Carr had gone.

He was accustomed to instructions of this kind. As there wanted three quarters-of-an-hour to the train time, he felt to be comparatively at leisure, so he decided to return home for a bag. He jumped into a cab.

As he re-entered the street which he had but just left in the company of Saloway, the subject of their conversation again possessed him. The elder man's attitude had touched all that was generous in Theodore, and the aspirations of mere egoism were for the moment eclipsed. To reduce Emily and her father to the position of pensioners only, seemed impossible to his uncompromising instincts.

Their services to him had been personal, so should be his to them. With that he strode into the house.

He went into the room they called the parlour, not expecting to find Emily there, but just within the doorway she confronted him.

' What is it, Theodore ?'

' I have to catch the ten o'clock train, and want my bag—but what——'

' I'll get it you in an instant.'

Emily tried to push impetuously past him, but he caught her by the hand, and turned her round to him. Her face was disfigured with weeping, and as he stared at her, she burst into tears afresh.

'Let me go, Theodore—you'll m—miss your train.'

'I don't care if I miss a thousand trains,' he asserted, 'I shan't let you go. What is the matter, darling?'

'I—I don't know; nothing; let me go.' And she passed him.

During the minute or two that she was absent, Carr stood in a reflective mood. Then hearing her step, he turned. She had commanded some greater degree of composure, but that it was merely enforced Theodore readily supposed.

Despite her entreaty that he would leave her, that he would miss his train, Carr took her hand and held it.

'Now, Emily, I must know before I leave you. Do you always spend your mornings like this?'

'No,' she said, a faint smile breaking over her features.

'Then why to-day? You asked me once

what was the matter with me, and I told you. Now we will change sides.'

'Really, Theodore, it is nothing. You didn't know what caused your trouble, and I don't know what caused mine. I felt wretched, that's all.'

His eyes rested upon her in ardent scrutiny, and possibly she felt something of their warmth.

'Go,' she muttered, pushing him playfully away.

'Yes, I will; but I will know when I come back, mind that.'

He placed his arm round her with sheltering strength, and, pressing her to his breast, kissed her twice, thrice, fully upon the lips,—kisses such as Emily had never felt before, from him or from anybody : kisses such as Carr had never given. Then he loosed her and leaped into the cab.

Theodore travelled in a state of exceptional turmoil that day,—exceptional for late days. His abandonment of all for that honest instinctive wave of sentimental emotion appeased certain cravings in him, but he was not long in finding that it created gaps in other directions. A dark suspicion of self-sacrifice crept up from the horizon and brooded over him; of ideals shattered which of late had constituted life. Strange visions had haunted him recently, which this impulsive act had scattered to the winds. He knew that in those kisses he had given to Emily his soul; he knew that she knew it. Retreat from that, now, could not for an instant occur to him; but he knew that it chronicled a loss. The swell of victorious joy which he was aware ought to attend such achievement sounded too much like derisive laughter—from those spirits which had gone. Fair brows, darkened with contemptuous frowns of upbraiding, hovered round him all the way, and he had to confess that he owned no weapons to dispel them. They allured him even whilst they despised; their taunts pierced wounds into his soul to which the soft glances of Emily could afford no balm.

That it was so could not be laid to Emily's charge. If the prayers and benedictions of a pure and tender woman can have efficacy for the sons of men, then ought Emily's to have availed Carr that day. From the moment that his lips had imprinted consecration upon hers, he was never off her soul for an instant. The dawn had startled and surprised her, but only in the overwhelming of her joy. She was dazed by the unexpected brilliance.

When Saloway came home to his dinner at midday, he saw the difference in his daughter, but it only added weight to his burden, and his mind was already taxed enough. The father's cloud, however, could not overspread the girl. She did not feel warranted in yet disclosing her hidden source of light, but she herself continued to bathe and flutter in the radiance. It had transfigured her world. The cobbler would not —nay, physically, could not speak, and speedily departed. His only respite was in toil. For two days this state of things continued; this juxtaposition of darkness and light. Emily's efforts were all unavailing; she had never been confronted by such extremity of gloom. The spectacle of her father passing silent from night to night recalled dark, dim visions of her childhood, which she had long thought dead. Even she began to feel oppressed.

On the third morning came a letter from Theodore,—a brief note addressed to Emily. It thrilled her with ecstasy for what she considered its tender close. He had to go on to Ireland, he said, and should probably be absent for a week. A week! Emily's heart sank at such an age of expectancy. She told her father with some characteristic comment. He looked straight at her as she said it, and for the first time in her life she was frightened by his eyes.

'What—— ?'

'Then I do it,' exclaimed the man, in a harsh guttural tone which did little to compose her.

'Do what, father?'

'I'll tell you at dinner-time, maidie,' he replied, in a softer tone. 'Be brave; your mother was.'

With that poor Emily had to sustain the morning—a morning of the darkest surmise. But the dinner-hour came, and Benjamin was true to his promise.

The dinner was spread, but neither seemed to

pay regard to such claims. The needs and expectations of both were gathered in their eyes, and these met as the cobbler entered. He went straight up to the outspread table, and placed a small canvas bag upon it. It was tied round with tape, and Emily heard, as she supposed, the clinking of coins within it. Saloway placed his hand upon his forehead.

'There be two hundred pounds, Emily, and a few odd ones. You wouldn't ha' thought I could have saved so much.'

'I shouldn't,' faltered the girl, incapable even of hazarding what this might portend.

'The furniture is mostly Theodore's,' Saloway went on, throwing his eyes around the room and over the table: 'except the few bits as we brought in . . . not a deal, not a deal.'

'What *do* you mean, father?' said Emily, going up to him and laying her hands upon his coat in definite alarm.

'I be a-going to leave this place to-morrow morning . . . Sit 'e down, Emily,' he continued, in an unsteady voice, 'and I'll tell you all as there be in my mind. We shall both want a deal of courage, but there be help other than the help of this world, and reward too, thank God, it 'ud be a poor affair for some at last else. We be a-hindering Theodore, do you see ? And I swore as I'd never stand in his way, come what might; no more I would, oath or no oath, all's one. He ben't one of we, clear enough; and it do hinder him most dreadful to live with the like o' we. So I be a-going, that be the upshot o' the matter.'

Emily was so far from comprehending the real points of the disclosure that she remained mute.

'He won't go, so we must. The goodness of the boy be against him, and there never was a better, never. Only the morning as he went away did I beg him to leave we to ourselves, as children that get on always do, of course,— he could come and see us and all, and I promised as I'd take money and things from him just to calm him, do you see? but he 'udn't; he changed in a minute.'

'That shows, father, that you are all wrong,' said Emily, collecting herself somewhat. 'He knows best.'

'That's where it is, Emily; he do, sure enough, but he 'unt do it. His heart be too good; it keeps him back, although he be awanting most despert to get forward. That be just the item. I've seen it long enough, more's the pity. He be a-sacrificing himself to we. If he 'ud go his own road it 'ud be right enough, but he wunt; and it be just that as makes the clouds come over him so.'

'Are you going away from him—to hide, and not let him know where you are?' cried the girl, aghast as the real meaning of her father dawned upon her.

Benjamin gave a solemn affirmative.

'But he loves—us,' Emily began, when the tears checked her, and she buried her face.

Saloway got up and moved about the room. He had, of course, foreseen this, endeavoured to prepare himself for it. But how ineffectual the preparation. For Emily alone now was he suffering; to sustain her was his only care.

'Mine be the fault, Emily,' confessed the man, bitterly, as he walked to and fro. 'I'd ought to ha' done it before; but I kept hoping. I never could be a man, and I've tried ever so. It be hard for you, maidie, cruel hard. But, look 'e, Emily,'—Saloway stopped, and put his hand upon the bent head of his daughter,—' do you hear, little maid? It be better now than later. Don't you see how he have been a-trying to draw himself off from you? If he have loved you one day, he have repented of it the next. It be a sorry start, Emily, when that comes at the first, I can promise you. Not that Theodore 'ud ever do wrong to you, very far from it; but after a bit it 'ud come over him. He'd feel as he ought to ha' done better, and oh, dear, it 'ud be a black day at the last. Very like it 'ud kill him, Emily, for he be like that. Don't you see what a gentleman he be? All his mind be on it. He do go on and on. He made as it were for me that he had that notion about leaving off the cobbling; but it were only as he didn't like it himself. Them as feel like that, don't. He'd grow ashamed o' you, Emily, after a bit; he couldn't help himself. Oh, I can see it all, but I be a bad hand at talking: ever have been since I saw the last o' Winwold.'

The cobbler paused, hoping that some of his words had reached their destination. The girl made no sign to show that it was so.

'It be for him, do you see, maidie? You wouldn't do harm to he?'

'But he has changed, father,' sobbed Emily. 'I know he has changed.'

'Not a deal. It be constant change with him, of course, because of his kind heart. He can't abide to think as he must separate from we. It be for we to do it, do you see, for his good, come what may; and if not, there be worse behind.'

A deep silence followed. Then Emily looked up and faced her father.

'Yes, we will go, father. Perhaps it is what you say.'

This wholly unexpected heroism brought Saloway a wave of encouragement, and he dared again to look forward.

'He will find us,' was the refrain that had inspired Emily.

With it ever ringing about her, she was able to sustain the preparations for their departure, which, as Saloway had intimated, was to be effected the next day, and effected it was accordingly.

Theodore returned a day short of his week. Although the change and movement attending his journey had been favourable to his condition, by enforcing external objects upon the eye and mind, he nevertheless had found no deliverance from the problem agitating him. One thing remained certain, and one thing only; all beyond was indistinct through flame. He came back to pledge his heart to Emily.

He reached Millington in the twilight, and took a cab home. He stepped out, paid the driver, and then turned to open the gate, which creaked exactly as it had always done. The blinds in the bow windows remained up, (a requirement of Emily's,) but no features were printed upon the glass to greet the traveller's return. His heart beat fast as he cleared the steps to the door; he tried it, but it was fastened. They did sometimes drop the latch, so he gave the short ring which would be enough to announce him. He heard a voice behind, and facing, distinguished the figure of a neighbour,—a widow of their friendly acquaintance.

'Here is the key, Mr. Carr. They asked me to give it you as they have gone out.'

'Oh,' was Theodore's involuntary exclamation as he took the key. 'Thank you, Mrs. Crowder,' he added, lightly. 'Are you pretty well?'

'If you would like to come in to have tea with me——'

'No necessity, thank you,' laughed Carr. 'The fire will be in. I shall be all right.'

The neighbour seemed desirous of saying more, but Carr had unlocked the door, and was entering; so she withdrew, sympathetically curious.

Once inside the house alone, Theodore felt the full force of his astonishment. Just distinguishing something on the oil-cloth, he took it up and found it a letter. His own, no doubt, fallen through the letter-hole and left lying there. Striking a match, he saw that it was so. They must have been absent then since early morning. Strange! He lit a gas-jet and looked about him. All was the same, but the silence fell upon him as distinctly ominous. What on earth was the meaning of it? He went first to the kitchen : silent and dark. Striking another match, he saw that the fire was laid, the hearth-stone and fender spotless, and all the room in unused order. His heart beat louder as he turned back again, and, without knowing why, he called out 'Emily!' Poising his head to listen, he thought the house seemed unusually hollow as the sound died away and silence fell. Therewith he walked into the parlour. A light came in from a gas-lamp just outside, and all looked the same. A ray directly struck the table, and revealed something white which lay on the crimson cloth. It was another letter, and, taking it into the passage, Carr saw that, upon the envelope was written, in the cobbler's handwriting, 'For Theodore Carr.' Here, then, was the solution of the mystery, but it was some seconds before he had courage to open and re-ceive it. The bottom post of the bannisters against which he leaned creaked, and was answered by another up the stairs. A cat mewed at a neighbouring doorway, and there were the footsteps of a passenger outside. A gate moved and the footsteps came nearer, but they went to the adjoining house. Theodore could hear the latchkey put in, the door open and close, a voice, another door close, and all was again still. Then he rent open his letter.

'DEAR THEODORE,

'We be gone for good. I have seen it long a-coming, but I had hoped as we might be spared. Don't be put about, for I have got two hundred pounds and above; and I be a-going to buy a little business with it as will keep us well. Forgive me for having hindered you so long. It was 'bliged to come. Go on and get a great rich man, and perhaps we shall meet again. God bless you for all the good you have done to both of we, and for all as you meant to do. But it will be a deal better so.

'Your loving

'B. SALOWAY.'

There was no addition by Emily.

Theodore stared and stared at the paper until he could see it no more, then he wept.

About an hour later he went and took up his quarters at an hotel.

CHAPTER VIII.

THE QUEST.

THE flight of Saloway brought Carr's conflicting instincts to an issue which might otherwise have been indefinitely postponed. That the cobbler and his daughter had some moral claim upon himself as well as upon any mere means that he might acquire was an impression from which Theodore could not easily escape. It was this morbid conception of gratitude that came continually to check his loftiest aspirations, as Benjamin had only too shrewdly supposed.

Whatever may have been the nature of Carr's devotion to Emily, it was clearly not the inevitable impulse of his being wherein lay the supreme achievement of his ideal life. Whenever he regarded it calmly it was invested with the same sense of sacrifice as it had ever been, and Theodore was by no means actuated by the heroic philosophy which acknowledges self-sacrifice for its highest goal. Nor was merely self-gratification the end of Carr's flight. There was a certain imaginative enthusiasm about his scheme of life ; a certain disinterested regard for what he deemed the elevation of mankind. He knew creative pride in his own development, and through it he could not but feel that he was advancing the highest destiny of his race.

Still, whatever one's intellectual theory, blunt human nature will constantly step in. It was thus inevitable that Carr should at this juncture be plunged into a gulf of distress and self-condemnation. All his attempts at pursuit proved futile, and he had to give them up. Therefrom, in mere oblivious despair, he plunged into the dissipations of the town. He spent hours where the glare of life (or is it the dance of death?) was fiercest. Into hitherto dark and forbidden corners he fearlessly peeped, finding strange and unexpected allurements in the recesses. The consequence was that in a week he was seriously ill.

He sent a note to his employer, and the latter came to him in his bed. Firkins expressed astonishment at finding him in the hotel, and the situation was explained. The cobbler's parting words were put into his hands.

'It has been long enough coming,' said the merchant, with brutal bluntness, throwing a swift glance at Carr. There was a glow of sinister triumph on the features of Mr. Firkins, and at that moment Theodore loathed him. After bidding him get well with speed, Firkins departed, and an hour later Carr received a case of port-wine with these words, 'Here is some '43. Get *that* into your head.—S. F.'

The timber merchant was in a state of fierce elation for a day or two. He did not love Carr; had never loved anybody in the whole course of his career, latterly upon principle; but his system needed Carr, and he viciously resented the intrusion of any other person between them.

In about ten days Carr appeared, although, as Firkins said to him, 'he didn't look up to much.' After the usual consultation upon the business of the day, the elder said,

'Have you heard anything?'

Carr had not.

'Well, I've inquired through the police for you. He has left the town.'

'So I supposed.'

'It is not known where he has gone. Is there anything else you want to know?'

Carr, not contemplating confidence in this man, affected to dismiss the matter lightly. The other's eyes gleamed.

'Now you're reasonable. What was that man to you? . . . Theodore looked away. Firkins stepped up to him, and clapped his iron hand upon the youth's shoulder. 'Look here, my boy—will you be my partner at five hundred a-year?'

Carr's frame trembled from head to foot, and he could not find a word. Firkins frowned.

'Well?' said the latter, fiercely.

'My work would not be worth that.'

'I don't give money,' grinned the master. 'If you were not worth it I should not offer it. Yes or no?'

'Certainly I accept it.'

'Then we'll have the agreement signed in a day or two, and in the meantime you go into the country to put some flesh on. If you send me your address, I can wire when I want you.' And Theodore was dismissed.

For the rest of the day Carr was in the greatest agitation, and he was unable to throw off a harassing fit of indecision. In the evening he met a musical acquaintance in the street. The man chanced to be seeking Carr with a view to carry him off to a great orchestral celebration in the Town Hall that night. They stopped, talked, and Theodore demurred. Ill-health,—only out of bed a day or two,—was going out of town.

'Humbug,—this is the very thing to put life into you. Time for dinner at Sampson's, and Town Hall in half-an-hour.'

Carr's arm was seized, and he was carried off to the restaurant in spite of himself.

As they sat at their table, hastily consuming viands for which they had scant time, Theodore felt the glow of life return. The sound and the glitter appealed to him. He took up his glass, and, looking through the wine, drank it. Carr liked wine; it had a generous suggestion. At the moment it occurred to him that he might always drink it, and of no despicable vintage too. Five hundred a-year! Could he not also the more easily find and help *them*? That night his mind flashed further into the depths of music than was its wont, and he talked vivaciously. Irresolution was no more. The armour with which he had dallied fitted him at last.

The following day Carr went off to Winwold, and established himself again at the ' Frog Mill Inn.' He had a definite intention in once more seeking these idyllic haunts wherein the highest peak of human life had been revealed to him. Beneath all the commotion of recent months he had been persistently conscious of Winwold as a creed, and of the girlish sprite Laura Blakenhurst as its divinity: nay, did not the unrest distinctly arise out of such essential revelation? The glory of it had oppressed him, by reason of his conscious need and of the hopeless remoteness of its achievement. To his sanguine eye much was now altered, and contemplation of the dazzling eminence became a practical inspiration rather than a quixotic melancholy. Ignoble, no doubt, but Carr breathed free.

It will be seen that Carr was not what we call in love with Laura at this time. She was much more of an intellectual than a sexual or emotional conception to him, but at the same time only a feminine nature could have inspired such as he with this poetic religion to which he was pledged. To gain him, it must hold out the sentimental possibility, however vague and insubstantial the immediate premises. Even his five hundred a year did not delude him into the absurdity of seeking the affections of Laura, even in remote imagination. All that it had done was to confirm him in the resolution of making himself personally compatible with such affections. Literally as 'a liberal education' had Laura manifested herself to him, and to such end he came again to behold and to contemplate her.

As he roamed the mellow autumn fields in reflective idleness, he found all the former enthusiasm in the mere joy and ambition of life restored to him. From the eminence to which circumstances seemed determined to thrust him, he could even regard the flight of Saloway with jocularity, so simple would his discovery of them be, and so princely the provision which he would make for their material welfare. From the trammels of personal bondage he was finally freed, for his enlarged income put his advance beyond the bounds of merely sanguine speculation, and every movement brought into more prominent relief the duty rather than the selfish preference which lurked in the chosen path. Saloway had truly discerned it, and to his terms Theodore was now ready to submit.

Even he at length perceived morbid infirmity of judgment. It was obvious from the highest ethical standpoint that his duty to Saloway was even scrupulously discharged by an affectionate intercourse with his early benefactors and a liberal care of their material wants. Even for Emily . . . He had viewed the world narrowly, immaturely; it was inevitable. Five hundred a year enabled him to get a broader glimpse of it. He lamented, nay, felt genuine distress at that impulsive display of tenderness towards her. No syllable of justification would he offer for such a painful lapse. But, fully admitting the shame of it, was it not well that it had gone no further? Carr had come to see a *duty* in what he deemed the progress of all his faculties. In this connection spectral fears hovered round the thought of marriage with Emily. What would have been her ¦predicament under the exactions (intellectual as much as material) of affluence? And what would have been his through her? The answer was clamorous and final.

Although eager in obtaining surreptitious glimpses of Laura, Carr was especially cautious to avoid another interview with her, as also to escape even her distant observation. This necessitated perilous manoeuvres in one or two instances, since it chanced at this time that Miss

Blakenhurst and her governess were addicted to rambles similar to his own, in order to command privacy for their high discussions.

Laura's intellectual development was proceeding consistently. As has been previously stated, her energetic nature could not rest upon theory. Girl though she was, what she felt, she must put in action; and thus it arose that a new and strange element had birth in the Blakenhurst family. In this young girl's brain no less a project than the reorganisation of the entire ancestral estate upon more or less socialistic, or at least philanthropic, lines established itself, and by stealth Laura forthwith commenced upon the fringe of her benevolent purpose. The old-world agricultural village, already very much overpopulated for the changing methods and conditions of husbandry, gave her ample scope. Her own pocket-money was abundant, and it soon came that nine-tenths of this was secretly expended on behalf of her unwashed neighbours. Not one half of the inhabitants professed any regular employment; their constitutional sluggishness therefore was promoted by inactivity so as to preclude wholly, not the power only, but the wish of attaining other more accommodating fields.

Carr, of course, in his idyllic construction of *la vie primitive* perceived nothing of this: the insight which Saloway's conversation had afforded being now blunted by the reflection that since the cobbler's day conditions were much altered. It was therefore with as great a sense of astonishment as of tremulous ecstasy that Theodore one day heard from Laura's own lips *her* idea of the situation.   At the time of the disclosure Laura suspected nothing of the addition to her audience, so that she played her part with characteristic energy and completeness.

It was from the mellowing foliage of a gigantic wych-elm tree that Theodore reaped this startling happiness, a shelter to which his musing temper occasionally led him.   In it he had found a comfortable couch, whereon he could lie in strictest concealment, and abandon himself to the tapping of the wood-pecker overhead, and the various movements of the horse by the trunk beneath ; revelling in that seductive annihilation ' of all that's made to a green thought in a green shade.' The bough upon which he lay hidden at the point where it separated from the parent trunk, some twenty feet from the ground, made a pendulous sweep downwards, and when within a few inches of the earth, rose again to expand into its leafy extremities. Carr, of course, was not aware that from childhood this had been a favourite tryst of Laura's under the name of the Swinging Tree. Singularly thrilling, therefore, was the emotion with which he awakened from his reverie to the consciousness of her magic tones beneath him. He moved some leaves that he might see her, and thus, with lips apart and pulse galloping, he did not scruple to devour with avidity every syllable that issued from so divine a source.

'Impossible, dear Laura ; wholly impossible,' said Miss Birdwell, the attendant governess.

'Nothing right and true can be impossible,' retorted the youthful sibyl.

'Not in the abstract, to be sure, but this world is a place of compromise. You must know that one syllable of this suggestion to your father, and the whole ceases.   He would not scruple to dismiss you from his doors penniless, and then what would become of your schemes, nay, of your very existence?'

'My schemes and my existence are proof against poverty,' proudly exclaimed Laura.

'That I fully believe, my dear; but it would curb them disastrously.   You could not do one jot of the good you do now, and this sense of inability would madden you.   Whereas if you patiently endure a compromise until you are older——'

'Oh, your old stock arguments!   But you can't feel the shame and disgrace of it.   It is my duty to convince my father of the gross degradation which such management involves him in.   Management! . . . chaos and savagery call it.   Think of the duties, or the mere glorious opportunities of his position.   What a place this might be!'

'Yes, Laura, and will be, if you proceed with caution.   You have heard your father's opinions; you must know him by this time.   Remember the story of Saloway.   He has not altered.'

'Do not insult and infuriate me, Miss Bird-well,' cried Laura, in such a tone that Carr moved his head so as to watch her more narrowly. 'If you mention that name again, all persuasion will be useless. That story would justify a crusade, though it *is* my father who is the Saracen.'

Theodore saw the flashing eye and the heightened colour which but the name of Saloway had been able to awaken, and his own composure was further imperilled by the generous display. His own reconciliation of adverse appearances in this old scandal flashed across him, and he blushed.

'In my opinion that very name should be the strongest inducement to patience,' returned the governess. 'In such a matter, violence would be childish. With patience, even the cobbler's fate may be atoned for—to his class, if not to the sufferer personally.'

A rook called as he alighted on the top of the tree, and Laura, reflecting, threw her eyes up in that direction, meeting as she little thought another pair amidst those lowest leaves. Carr trembled, so impossible in face of such a gaze did it seem that he was effectually hidden. But the lowering of Laura's face proved his fears groundless.

'I suppose it is so,' she muttered, and therewith at a bound leapt on to the swinging bough beside which she had been standing, and caught a branch above to serve her as a trapeze. After swaying to and fro thus suspended by her hands, she flung herself some distance forward, and alighted gracefully on her feet.

'Come, then, let us mount the Knapp,' said Laura, and as she led the way up the green slope, Theodore's eyes rested in fervid enthusiasm upon the retreating figure, until it was finally lost behind a great clump of gorse.

Even then his attitude and the expression of his features did not alter, so great was the effect of the incident upon him. In place of the actual figure which had just appeared and vanished, he was gazing into a dazzling futurity which that figure so brilliantly typified, and in the golden haze of which every emotion of his soul was now aglow. The physical glory of the figure and the music of the voice only intensified impressions previously made upon Carr's sensibility, but the significant tenor of the girl's words created something wholly new. The revelation surprised, overjoyed, even in some subtle respects reconciled Carr. It had afforded him an entirely new clamp to his armour which, to one so given to self-inspection, rendered yeoman's service.

Although Theodore's capitulation to the new creed had been by no means wholly an ignoble one, this clear confirmation of the germ of continuity with the old one was none the less gratifying, and served to bring out the world for which he was bound into more distinct relief. To the merely sensual allurements of wealth he had never succumbed. All his aspirations were intellectual, spiritual. Every dollar that he was amassing did but increase his power of acquiring and of diffusing light. Money as money was utterly repugnant to his instincts. It was grace, beauty, love—the essence of all highest art and life—that alone it held for him. That it *should* contain unbounded, systematic benevolence also he had firmly resolved, he now knew that it might and did contain it. Long he gazed at that brilliant horizon through the framework made by the leaves around.

From this moment Carr accepted his quest as an irrevocable aim of life, for which he must equip himself with almost religious enthusiasm. Indeterminate personal elements took substance, and the youth confronted them fearlessly. No longer was Laura Blakenhurst *only* an ideal source of abstract inspiration in this lofty enterprise; that she was still, and of course always must be, but in addition she was concrete woman for whom the man Theodore Carr knew human need. This was perceived and acknowledged to be an essential part of the quest, and gradually around it all central speculation and hope began to cluster. By its light even the prosaic daily round became transfigured, and Carr could think of his commercial work not with tolerance only, but with aggressive zeal. Laura was so young yet, in that fact lay his only solid encouragement. How much could he not get into the years still allowed him,

before it would be so much as seemly to connect the full womanly fragrance with her un-
folding nature! . . . But Theodore loved her,
and knew that he loved her as aspiring man
loves inspiring woman.

So impatient for activity did this reflection
make him, that he leaped down from his concealment and strode impetuously towards the
village. What had been his strongest impulse
to poetic reverie became suddenly a goad to
feverish work. The country calm disturbed instead of solacing him, and he resolved to quit
it without awaiting his senior's summons . . ?
Work!

That evening accordingly saw him again in
Millington.

CHAPTER IX.

THE FAIR ENIGMA.

Two or three years passed in uneventful, if not insignificant, development. Baffled in his early strenuous efforts to trace the fugitive Saloway and his daughter, Carr imperceptibly concurred in what seemed marked out as the inevitable. It is not of course likely that such conclusion ever took definite form in his mind. His life was so full of that one unalterable purpose to which all the world was reduced that all else simply lapsed,—was overgrown by the march of circumstance,—until his association with the homely cobbler faded to the recollection of a ray from a last year's sunset.

Laura Blakenhurst as a positive aspiration now dominated Carr's career. Romantic as his original conception of her had of necessity been, he was now able to recognize the conventional needs of practical life, and he reduced his scheme to almost commonplace terms. In pursuance of a chivalrous regard for womanhood, as much as with an eye to the supposed requirements of his own personal culture, Theodore resolved to lay no siege to Laura before she should have completed her twentieth year. It was his determination to present himself to her eye as in every sense a creation worthy of so transcendent a gaze.

Such lofty aim imposed upon Carr a dignity and gravity of demeanour not common in one of his years. It involved also a certain exclusiveness towards his commercial neighbours which many resented, and which led still more to inquire by what authority the orphan pauper had become so inordinate a prig. The man persistently declined all part in strictly municipal affairs, but in any social or intellectual movement he remained active. This imaginative outlook was but a natural consequence of the association of idyllic conditions with the aims in which he was engaged. If Laura was still the divinity, Winwold, her natural setting, was still the creed. This was the type of highest existence, just as she was the crown of life. Pastoral literature and art therefore possessed him, and his means now permitted him full indulgence of his tastes. These personal ideas led him to propound to one or two municipal magnates a scheme for a Fine Art Gallery under public auspices, and he had the satisfaction of seeing the suggestion ultimately adopted. He was invited to co-operate, and gained much consideration by his knowledge and address.

To this undertaking Carr devoted much of his spare time, and by giving so definite an outlet to his imaginative energies, it lightened the restraints of his commercial life. It, moreover, brought him a congenial friend in the person of the keeper who was appointed to the chair of authority in the institution, a gentleman of taste and artistic learning, who, to his other good qualities, united the frank geniality of an enthusiast. Under such influences Carr's horizon widened, and he got further from the introspective meshes that had once threatened him. Nor was this all.

Coming to the gallery one day as was his custom, Theodore was seized by the curator with characteristic manifestation of high mystery.

'Come along,' was all to be got from him until they were in that gentleman's sanctum, when, 'Now, then, wait a minute,' was added by the spectacled critic with great profundity of tone.

Carr looked on amused, whilst a picture, which had been turned to the wall, was fetched from a corner.

'A new man, sir. David Cox and Morland in one, not without a strain of J. M. W. T. Nothing less, you understand.'

The speaker held the treasure behind him, with an arch glance which he had preserved from childhood.

'His name? . . . You wouldn't know it . . .

Bah, none of us know it . . . but—look there !'

It was a small picture of a pastoral kind. An upland pasture, gorse-dotted in the noonday sun, as a ridge against the fair clouded sky crowned by a clump of fir-trees planted on a small mound, the sides of which were hollowed by the sheep to lie in. It was not sheep but cows which figured in the present picture, on the mound between the tree-trunks. You saw that the standing animals faced the summer breeze, and the movement of tail and fore-foot was admirably rendered. But, faithful as was all this, Carr felt that it was the breeze and open sunlight of the wold that the artist intended for him, and a thrill as of religious ecstasy passed over him at the suggestion.

'Yes, that is good,' said he, with noticeable restraint.

'It is great. A man to have passed the age of forty in doing such work, and us not to know of him !   "Fillip me with a three-man beetle." Oh, Carr, it is criminal !   The free breath on the sky-line, man !'

'It is like a breath from Winwold,' mused

Carr, audibly, scarcely knowing that he spoke until his companion's clutch was upon his shoulder and his tragic stare upon his face.

'You know him, you reprobate!'

'Indeed I do not,' laughed Theodore. 'Why so?'

Pacing the room, the enthusiast explained. The artist lived at Winwold; worked in seclusion there, exhibited nowhere; had an exclusively private connection. A Mr. Nevison had presented them with this precious specimen of his skill, or else they had continued in Cimmerian darkness still.

'But now, come, *you* explain,' cried he, in conclusion, confronting Carr with suspicious eye. 'Where *is* this Winwold?'

Carr gave in quite general terms his knowledge of the locality, and an expedition thither for the following Sunday was speedily arranged, the patron, Mr. Nevison, being relied upon for the necessary credentials.

It was about two years before that this artist, Henry Lindred by name, had established himself at Winwold, in an ancestral farm-house called Farbarrow, somewhat removed from the village, and it was to this retreat that Carr and his friend repaired upon that particular Sunday. Carr naturally made the pilgrimage with much perturbation. Although he had ministered to his spiritual needs by frequent journeys to Winwold, he had not as yet established any social relationship there. He saw therefore, at a flash, several elements of importance in this projected intercourse with a gentleman of Lindred's position which came opportunely, and which this first visit did not serve to dim.

In the early autumn sunlight, beside a bed of sunflowers and hollyhocks, the visitors first beheld the artist with his pipe. He bade them welcome before reading the letter they had brought; afterwards he at once put them upon a footing of refined familiarity. Mr. Lindred's daughter, a girl of sixteen, joined them, and in company they all traversed the garden to confirm their acquaintance by the test of small talk.

The confirmation was supreme; Carr at once giving himself up to the glory of the situation

with characteristic fervour. The subtle properties of the atmosphere stimulated ideals, nay,
schemes of his own, and gave to them an actuality
which to long-protracted fancy was peculiarly
grateful. Judging by this first glimpse of him,
Lindred had attained to that rare intellectual
summit wherein spiritual and material life becomes one appropriate artistic whole. Since the
death of his wife, the artist lived only for his
daughter and his art,—the latter of which he
accepted in a comprehensive spirit more typical
of earlier times. To earlier centuries also belonged his inherent placidity of soul, the rays
of which seemed to penetrate smaller mortals as
they looked into his eyes. To Carr they were
a new source of highest inspiration, and he invoked them continually. This strong secret
sympathy must have been soon perceived by
Lindred, and in some measure accepted and
reciprocated, for a distinct personal kindliness
was rapidly displayed in the artist's behaviour
towards Carr.

The afternoon thus sped swiftly, until tea in
the studio was announced.

In a spirit of reverence, worthy of true pilgrims, did the visitors enter here. Carr's eyes travelled quickly round the walls, you might have thought with definite purpose, but they were recalled complacently, and he took the oak stool which Dorothy playfully brought out for him. She always read instinctively her father's construction of visitors, and adapted her behaviour to them accordingly. The predominence of her natural fun was a sign of highest compliment which Carr was courtier enough to perceive. Moreover, Dorothy's independent judgment readily confirmed her father's taste in this case, for Theodore presented such modified aspect of manhood as was peculiarly agreeable to the simpler types of feminine nature. It was therefore Carr who assisted the young hostess in her duties at the tray.

Mr. Lindred and his other visitor perambulated the studio, scraps of their conversation coming over to the other two in their lighter sallies, which perhaps caused Carr's occasional glance in their direction.

'It is rather too bad, father, that Mr. Carr's

good-nature should exclude him from the view of your masterpieces,' said Dorothy, in quick recognition of her companion's glances. 'He is assiduously placing cups for you.'

'Mr. Carr wisely chooses the better part, Doss,' said the artist, in pretty compliment, turning as he spoke, with a small canvas in his hand. 'But we are at your command.'

Carr looked over to him, smiling, and in doing so his eye fell upon the picture which Mr. Lindred was putting down. The expression of Theodore's face suddenly altered, but in the general movement it was not observed. He, however, with quick control, cautiously secured himself behind a display of frankness as the artist came up.

'Striking features those even at a distance,' was his remark.

'That sketch . . . yes. I call it the "Fair Enigma,"' the artist said. 'You shall see it when Dorothy permits.'

They took up their cups, and the light talk became general. Dorothy, in playful pique, soon gave the needful permission by herself fetching the picture they had referred to, and rearing it upon the high mantelpiece that it might appear to preside over them all. Oddly enough a silence of several seconds' duration fell upon them as they looked upon what she had done.

'Well, father, it *is* lovely,' said the girl—the first who spoke.

Unlike the generality of Mr. Lindred's pictures there, it was a portrait, and, as all confessed, a striking one, apart from all knowledge of the original. Carr, indeed, pronounced it an imaginary creation of the artist's brain, but this was negatived. The picture was obviously in progress only, but many might have deemed the main features completed. Mr. Lindred said they were not so,—confessed his inability to complete them,—that for a twelve-month he had pondered the necessary strokes without success.

'It eludes me,' added he, addressing Carr. 'It is like the "glorious morning" of the sonnet, and I hesitate to pronounce upon the day.'

'But *that* morning can never permit the basest clouds to rise,' interposed Carr, in prompt interpretation of the allusion.

'You think not?' asked the artist, pleased. 'Basest . . . no; but some clouds?'

'It is not a human face otherwise,' was Theodore's philosophic response. 'That morning can only ¡permit majestic ones; massive glistening, noon-day clouds which heighten the beauty of the day, and give a record to the empty blue.'

'You think so?'

Mr. Lindred listened with undisguised attention to the young merchant's mind. Much as he had personally liked him, he mentally confessed that he had not looked for this fund of imagination. Carr's friend, the curator, also eyed him narrowly, and pronounced assent. Having by these few words gained complete command of himself, Theodore let his eyes rest fixedly upon the face they were discussing.

In general terms it was lovely, so Dorothy had said; but the clear depth of life within shone also there for such as might behold it. What to the poetical sense of centuries has been vaguely comprised in womanhood was not enough here. Domestic emotion by no means disposed of the forces suggested by Mr. Lindred's art. Perhaps there was justification for the mature artist's scruple in striking the balance. As Carr's enthusiasm, however, testified, a younger eye could have no doubt. To this, let the fulness of life there be what it might, it could not but be the effusion of the highest yet revealed to the human soul.

The topic thus casually raised led the company into deeper water than they had hitherto sounded this particular afternoon. The seriousness with which Carr took part in the discussion proclaimed the fact that contemplation of the female element in life was not now first presented to him. His artless fervour was peculiarly agreeable to Lindred, and the artist did not hesitate to show his appreciation of an ingenuous mind. Reception such as this stimulated Carr's faculties, and he rose to unwonted heights.

' Your opinion highly interests me, Mr. Carr,' said the artist, when they had got back to the text from which they had set out; ' and I hope you will allow me the opportunity of discussing it further with you. I am curious to know how a sight of the original would affect your judgment. You would not object to an interview upon neutral ground—here, for instance?'

'By no means,' laughed Carr, light-heartedly. 'I hope I should not be insensible to the honour. May I ask the lady's age?'

'Is that permissible, Doss?'

'There is certainly no secrecy observed upon the matter. She is——'

'But no,' cried the artist. 'Mr. Carr must guess that also.' And thus was the subject humorously disposed of.

It was noticeable that Mr. Carr discussed with just as brilliant a play of imagination the various landscape studies which engaged their attention for the remainder of their visit. In subjection to Sunday trains, (the station three or four miles away,) the visitors had to leave early.

Carr was in a state of extreme exhilaration throughout the return journey. His intellectual vivacity astonished his companions, even previous intimacy not having prepared him for quite so mature a display. Theodore had

purchased on his own behalf two of the land-
scapes which Lindred had on hand, and in the
train he opened them and throughout the hour's
ride descanted in a vigorous manner upon certain aspects of the art exemplified.

In the seclusion of his own room, too,
Theodore continued jubilant. His spirits were
not the fleeting effervescence of social contact merely. He was conscious of permanent
elation due to the miraculous advancement of
his plans. The life to which but a year or two
ago he had quixotically aspired was now positively within his clutch, it needing but a stretch
forward of his hand to make that highest craving
all his own. It is astonishing how seldom to the
genuinely sanguine man repulses are allowed.
His instincts are in league with fate, or else extort the decrees required. Instinct was now law
and fact to Carr, and everything seemed bent
upon a confirmation of this creed.

To and fro he paced before those two pictures
propped up on a couch. They were but tiny
fragments to be sure of the vast horizon he was
scanning, but they *were* fragments of it, and so

served to keep the whole vividly before his gaze. Over it, like a fair cloud crested with the morning rays, rose the enigmatic features which were imprinted on his heart,—enigmatic to the calculating world, clear and sufficing as those rays themselves to the soul for which they were created.

And Laura was now turned nineteen; therefore a sovereign glory in a world compact of glories—a woman, in soul and body, beautiful.

In the reflection to which this thought was tending, Theodore was checked. It was eleven o'clock, and all the house was still; the other inmates having retired to rest. Suddenly, in the quiet without and in, Carr heard hurried footsteps pass his window on the pavement outside. He paused to listen, he knew not why, and the door bell was loudly rung. So incongruous was any commonplace thought, that for a moment Carr was simply confused. When the bell again sounded, more violently than before, he recovered himself and went out into the hall.

CHAPTER X.

PROSE.

CARR only had his own rooms in the house, so that this untimely summons was not necessarily for him. Indeed, being a man of regular, almost methodic habits, and of the scantiest social relationships, the probability was that it was not, for even Firkins left him in peace on Sundays. Nevertheless, as the appeal had a ring of urgency in it, and as there were no immediate sounds above, Theodore went and unbolted the door himself.

'Is Mr. Carr here?' was flung in on the gust of night air before the door was fully open.

'Yes, I am——'

'Mr. Firkins wants you, sir, immediately.'

Carr bit his lip.

'At the Queen's?'

'Yes, sir, he has been ill all day.'

'Why, I saw him this morning. Nothing serious, is it?'

'Can't say, sir.' And with a promise of immediate attendance the messenger was dismissed.

Carr had often thought that the omnipotent merchant's erratic dealings with him were prompted occasionally by sullen caprice alone, and in view of such Theodore found that bare gratitude was capable of a strain. Indeed, since the flight of Saloway, Theodore had been conscious of a distinct personal antipathy towards his generous partner, which in one of Carr's complex temperament may not have been so incongruous an outcome of five hundred a year as at first sight it may seem to be. Human nature has various ways of appeasing its weaknesses, one of which may be an energetic intolerance of the agent that successfully plays upon the particular failing we are most anxious to repudiate. In his poetical apotheosis of mere wealth and the grim urgency of its immediate attainment, had it ever occurred to Carr that the bloom of his human virtue had been purchased from him in this hot pursuit of ideal good? Had he ever seen through the bald vista of a grey spiritless day, passengers along two diverging roads, not long parted company perchance, but already fronting very different journeys, the several horizons before them not varying more than the contrasted nature of their paths and the eyes with which they were able to regard them? There was little external evidence whereby to decide it; but had Theodore Carr at any time had so much as hint or glimpse of this, some counteractive emotion would undoubtedly be required of him.

At any rate, in the quietude of this Sunday night, Theodore threaded the empty streets in a state of rebellious agitation. That a man of Firkins's mould should have the power to summon him thus at any unreasonable moment by a single twirl of a finger was irritating enough; but in face of the mental attitude in which he had been surprised, the gross savour of the topic which was in prospect incalculably heightened the outrage. For the whole of this day had his mind been attuned to abstract things, to things immeasurably removed from the arid wastes to which the bulk of Carr's life was for the present condemned, and yet was this last hour to dispel the vision by its noisome touch. Upon the hotel steps Theodore recoiled, but there was a sound as of derisive scorn, and he looked around. Nobody else was there. Firmly commanding his lips, Carr went in.

A waiter informed him that Mr. Firkins had been seized dangerously ill, so Carr hurried upstairs forthwith. Firkins—ill! The mere suggestion came as such a startling absurdity that the remaining incidents could have but little effect upon Carr.

He entered the sitting-room which Firkins occupied, but found it empty. Pausing to consider, he heard in the next room his own name vociferated in the sick man's most ferocious humour. Unlatching that door, a strange sound was heard. There were quick, heavy breathings and the scuffling that might attend a personal conflict. Again his name was called, and Theodore stepped hastily in. All was quiet at once.

The scene presented in the gas-light struck Carr mute. Firkins sat up in bed as it seemed distraught. At one side of him was a man of middle-age, still holding the muscular invalid as though he had wrestled with him. The bed-clothes about them were lying in the utmost disorder. On a chair at the other side sat an old woman with features which bore a strong resemblance to those of Carr's benefactor as there presented. Her fixed eyes had travelled slowly from the bed to Theodore standing just within the doorway, and there remained.

'There's the man,' said Firkins, and fell back resignedly upon the pillow.

'Do you want a doctor?'

'Fetch the police.'

Carr turned mechanically to obey.

'There's no need of that. Come along, mother.'

The man, who had relaxed his hold of the merchant when Carr appeared, rose, and taking the old woman by the arm, went to the door.

'God forgive you, Sam,' muttered she, and they had gone.

So brief had been the unaccountable scene, so soon dispelled, and so normal all that follow- ed, that Carr, in such condition as he was, hardly grasped it as an actual occurrence. Firkins, although slightly out of breath, was at once collected, and spoke only of the commer- cial affairs that were on his mind.

'You must have a doctor, sir,' urged Carr.

'Will you listen to what 1 say?' roared Firkins; but, as it seemed, checked by some physical disturbance, (for there was an involun- tary contortion of his swarthy features,) his voice fell as he added, 'They have done with me, Carr. I have fought with this devil for years.' He then proceeded hurriedly with his financial injunctions.

Despite the vague alarm which was borne in upon him by the troubled atmosphere, it was scarcely possible for Carr to realise that this man, to whom from any point of view he owed so much, was confronting death. That he was in constant physical agony was only too apparent from the abrupt pauses in his speech, the uncertainty of his tones, and the suppressed muscular convulsions which all the man's superhuman efforts were unable to hide. Whatever Carr's previous feelings towards him, it was not possible for him to witness this unmoved. His former construction of Firkins's character only heightened the tragic element in what he saw. Nothing in that iron creature had ever suggested the mere mortal: it was impossible to connect with him anything but aggressive, preterhuman force. Something that had ever been and must ever be, so long as any part of the world's elemental rock remained. This had been in Carr's estimate of him whatever else was there; but now was he suddenly bidden to believe that this man must die. The whole of his nature was melted in a fierce unbounded sympathy. He himself loved life. His face showed the workings of his mind, and Firkins detected his inattention.

'Do you hear?' he cried once, with incipient anger.

'I hear, but can pay no heed,' promptly replied Carr. 'Do you think it possible for me to sit here and see you suffer without raising a hand to help you?'

'What can you do?'

'Fetch every doctor in the town. If one fails to cure you——'

'Come here, Carr.'—Firkins clutched his hand.—'Nobody has ever offered to do so much for me. I tell you that no doctor in the land could now help me. I have seen all the best of them in the world, and have by three years outlived the time they gave me. Do you believe me now?'

'I believe you, but will not believe that your case is hopeless. If you have outlived their time by three years, you may outlive it by three more. I shall fetch——'

'I will see three of them to satisfy you, but not one beyond. Send for them, but you stay here.'

Carr summoned an attendant and despatched messages to the three principal physicians in the town, he himself taking the chair which

Firkius indicated. From this moment Theodore could see that his companion's manner altered. Even a ray of human feeling seemed occasionally to glimmer through the chill cynical vapour that habitually obscured his face. Indeed, Carr's obviously disinterested sincerity had penetrated even this man in his prostration. It might have seemed as a direct result of this, Firkius's conversation underwent a change. All the urgent commercial schemes, which but a moment ago he had been so impatient to communicate, were forgotten, and for some seconds he lay in his bed quietly regarding Carr. When he spoke again, his subject was so ludicrously inconsequent that Theodore for a moment supposed him deranged.

'Did you ever forgive your parents, Carr?' demanded the merchant, without moving his eyes.

'Certainly, for everything they could possibly require pardon,' was the reply.

'And what was that?'

Carr admitted that he knew of no specific charge.

'I didn't think you were such a fool,' said Firkins, more sharply, which betrayed to Carr that the derangement was on his own side, or, at any rate, not on the other. 'Do you find the only thing they ever gave you so acceptable a gift?'

'I suppose I am a fool. I don't in the least understand you.'

'You saw that hag in the room just now—that was my mother.'

The tone in which the words were uttered horrified Carr, for they awakened at the same moment a vision of the only parent he had ever known, as she lay sleeping in the pea-field, and of whom he had ever thought with reverence and oppressive sympathy. He could not speak, but Firkins read his features.

'You think me a fiend—think it and welcome. "Honour thy father and thy mother," is that it, boy? It is well for me that my father I never knew, or else I should have honoured him so far as not to have been dying here in bed . . . In bed, heavens !' Firkins raised himself at a bound, and clenched his iron fist.

'What did they give me between them?' he
went on, with a diabolic grin. 'Life!' and he
smote his bare chest with a blow that might
have killed a man. 'This rotten trunk! A kennel for a bed, and for a plate the gutter, for life
. . . hell.'

Muttering the last word, the man sank upon
the pillow and stared at Carr.

'Would you be grateful for that?' he asked,
when the paroxysm was over.

'This is frightful,' returned Carr. 'Would
you saddle a fly of a mortal with all the grim
mysteries of the universe? Assault the heavens
if you like, but hasn't your own nature taught
you sympathy with your fellow worms?'

'Mysteries of the universe? . . . The heavens,
do you say?' mused Firkins, displaying in his
eyes the tragic effort that it cost to guide his
intellect. 'With the heavens I have nothing to
do. If . . . if you go by that . . . they'll tell
you that I came from hell . . . and that——'

Carr took the man's hand, and watched his
eyes again slowly open. There was something
that he strove to say, but beyond 'You are——'

indistinctly uttered, there was nothing articulate. A strange placidity gradually sank upon the hitherto unquiet features, and from the regularity of the breath, Theodore gladly perceived he slept.

In a few minutes the first doctor came.

'He was right,' said this gentleman to Carr. 'He has consulted everybody. None but *he,*—pointing to the silent figure—'could have fought it out so long.'

Some time later Theodore Carr retraced his steps through the quiet streets with yet new subjects of meditation to engage him.

CHAPTER XI.

NOON.

CARR had been early initiated into the mystery of death, but had woven nothing of the hideous into his conception of it. His temperament was far too buoyant to be highly speculative, therefore had he been able to accept the departure of the soul as merely a natural fact, in much the same way as he would accept an ordinary sunset. It was a sleep, with illimitable possibilities wrapt up within it. His last scene with Firkins had disturbed this healthy optimism by an obtrusion of mere charnel-house horrors upon him and an unnatural dejection overclouded his spirit in consequence.

So exclusively was Carr's instinct imaginative, that this high aspect of the event precluded all hint of the practical. Not so much as a thought of material good or harm to accrue to himself as a result of it for a moment assailed him. Only the abstract bearings upon the human soul of so horrible a disclosure were visible, and he was daunted. Nay, his mere commercial responsibilities vanished. At ten o'clock the following morning he was in bed, tracing ghastly legends across the ceiling, supremely oblivious of the world's demands upon Messrs. Firkins and Carr. An arrival of a message from the head clerk in his office failed to disturb him. Having scribbled an injunction to the man to do what was necessary and close the premises, he relapsed into his former abstraction and apathetic gloom, and thus he continued until noon.

The clock had not long struck twelve, when there was another knock, and another communication announced to him. This time he leaped up, and, throwing on a dressing-gown, took the letter in himself. It was addressed in a writing not familiar to him, and had not come through the post.   In going to receive it, some preposterous fancy had suggested Laura.   Now he was so unnerved that the envelope quivered in his hand, and in a fit of impatience he threw it to the floor.   When he had done so, there was another knock.

'Please, sir, an answer is wanted.'

'Answer wanted—to what?' shouted Carr.

'The letter.'

'Oh, yes.'

Carr snatched it up, and, having torn it open, saw that it was from Mr. Firkins's solicitor.   He requested an interview as soon as possible, whenever Mr. Carr might deem convenient.

'I'll be at his office in half-an-hour, say.'

When the footsteps had left the landing, Carr went to his bath, and under the enforced activity his mind regained much of its normal tone.

The lawyer confirmed the cure.   He received Carr with affability, whilst properly shocked at the sad occurrence they both deplored. In view of a mysterious visit he had that morning received, he had thought it advisable that they should at once confer upon executorship affairs. Carr of course would give every assistance in his power, but Mr. Firkins had never disclosed to him much of his concerns. But he would have spoken of his will? Not a word. The lawyer produced from a safe behind him a sealed envelope, and handed it to Carr. Theodore demurred.

'No hands but yours were to open it. You see, it is addressed to you.'

Under a return of that former agitation, Carr cut it open and took out the contents—a sheet of ordinary note-paper, at which even the law-yer stared. Theodore read it, and gave it to his companion, who also read :

'This is the will of Samuel Firkins, *nullius filius*, known to myself and a few others as a timber-merchant of the West Docks in Millington, Gloucester-shire, whereby I devise and bequeath the whole of my real and personal estate whatsoever, including the whole of my business and everything connected with it, to Theodore Carr, my partner, whom I also ap-point my sole executor. I suppose even by law I may do what I will with my own. I fought for every sixpence that ever I got, and thus I leave it.'

This document was in the testator's own handwriting, was dated, signed, and attested in due order. The lawyer, looking at Carr in silence, saw that all trace of colour had left his face, so he brought forth a chair.

'Is it effectual?' asked Theodore, as he sat down.

'By all means . . . but do you happen to know whether Mr. Firkins's mother is alive?'

'She was last night.'

'You would know her? . . . Very good. You would of course wish to make some provision for her?'

'Ample provision. Whatever you may think she would be able to make a right use of.'

'To be sure, to be sure. Some foolish man came here to-day, ostensibly an emissary of hers, but no doubt a trader upon his own account, threatening to contest any will that did not, etc. Should you hear of him, pray refer him to me.'

'Nothing more will be necessary to-day?'

'You do not forget funeral arrangements.'

'That devolves upon me! . . . You will

allow some clerk of yours to give all necessary instructions. I really cannot grapple with it myself . . . I have not had the remotest suspicion of all this.'

Thus it was arranged, and Carr took to flight, —nobody hearing anything about him until he stood beside the grave.

For some time after this Carr spent his days conscientiously immersed in the vast commercial imbroglio which had been Firkins's life, and with the mere fringe of which Theodore himself had been hitherto sufficiently employed. His nights he spent with himself.

When the young capitalist came fully to realize the extent of the business which that Titan had borne unaided upon his shoulders, he quailed before the fund of superhuman energy disclosed. Any attempt on the part of such dilettante faculties to cope with the intricacies of so stupendous a machine seemed ludicrous, and so for some days Carr felt it; but soon the challenge awakened his innate reserve of determination, and he took up the glove. The trnly sanguine man of general capacity is aware of no limit to his range, and, given the mood, will confront herculean tasks for which he might appear the least fitted. This propitious mood had been forced upon Carr just now. The sudden shock of the extraordinary complication of affairs occasioned by the timber-merchant's death had, for the nonce, extinguished Theodore's ideal life. The inundation had transformed the world, and he saw nothing but the sea of commerce around him. Darkness and chaos it naturally at first appeared, but in mere assertion of a strong vitality he at length struck out, and, after a period of frantic muscular contention, he became aware that he was afloat. This rapidly gave him strength to clear his eyes, and thereupon he saw that his own efforts had been enough to still the waters and dispel the night.

This strenuous exercise had a greater effect upon Carr than he himself imagined. The supreme exertion, and the victory attending it, had imposed such graduation in responsible manhood as no previous crisis in his life had done. He emerged from the engagement many years older, and bereft for ever of a certain purely idyllic strain which had hitherto entered into his view of things. He had seen the world a fact, and through whatever glow of imagination he might yet again regard it, at least a reality it must to the end remain.

Having mastered the difficulty, it was no part of Carr's intention to imperil his life by sustaining it. Although victor in the field, the prospect none the less appalled him, and he forthwith set about the terms of truce. As a first step he enrolled as his working partners two men in whom he had implicit faith; one an old and tried dependent of his own timber-yard, the other a man hitherto of smaller enterprise on his own account. He himself retained the post of commander-in-chief.

All the practical details of his succession Theodore conducted in a most liberal manner. His allies pronounced his behaviour princely, and so were bound to him. His method with himself was on a similar scale. For current use he realised the sum of twenty thousand pounds (Mr. Firkins, he found, had systematically refrained from realizing—the balance on his private banking account being under eighty pounds) and once again Carr found himself able to confront the world with a calm fearlessness of gaze. That haunting fiend of means was now finally laid—with the more agreeable *end* need he alone concern himself.

His intellectual reaction hereupon he found to be immense. What had been before horizons, were now infinities of space. Opportunity and capacity alike were boundless, and the man trembled to essay a flight. It must be admitted that his most sanguine expectations had not foreseen wealth at such an age and upon such terms as these. That he was born to acquire wealth we know he had never doubted; but in the acquisition he was prepared for years of uncongenial work—what the commercial mind calls work, the speculative parry and thrust of preternatural ingenuity and greed. Solely in the purposes for which he sought his wealth could Theodore Carr claim any distinction from the most rapacious gambler of us all. If he had ever deigned to limit his gaze to this particular point in ethics, it can scarcely have lingered long. Was he not on the current of the established world? So far in advance of it, indeed, as to know that his eye was fixed upon the light. Self-aggrandisement was by no means his farthest point.

It was in this exalted state that an invitation from Mr. Lindred reached him, and it seemed to lay the train of which Carr's excited energies had been in need. By a flash the combination of present facts with former ideals was accomplished, and Theodore was conscious of yet a fresh result. His reply to the artist was this :*

'DEAR MR. LINDRED,

'Only a state of mental and physical exhaustion prevents my immediate acceptance of your invitation. I have but just emerged from the swamp of most prosaic toils, and certainly find myself in anything but a fit condition for grappling with enigmas, fair or foul. 1 am on the eve of going abroad for two or three weeks (not more), and I trust that on my return (of which I shall take the liberty of informing

you) you will be able to find another opportunity of affording me the pleasure of a visit to
Farbarrow, my first glimpse of which lingers so
radiantly in my affections.   May I beg my com-
pliments to Miss Lindred, and remain,

'Most truly yours,

'THEODORE CARR.'

Of course there was a little innocent dissimulation in this calm response.   Until taking
the pen in hand to write it, Carr had had no
such determinate grasp of the situation, but
now that the needed inspiration had come, he
saw the real value of its light.   From that
momentous Sunday visit to Winwold, Mr. Lindred had unconsciously become a vital link in
Carr's highest affairs, and the artist's personality,
as shining through his letter, had prompted the
necessary comment upon a future course.   For
an instant it had appeared that Winwold was
Carr's present want.   Without any suspicion of
the fact, Mr. Lindred had assured him that it
was not.

The fact was, Carr had become suddenly

aware that his next appearance at Winwold
must inevitably be as an aspirant for Miss
Blakenhurst's hand ; a supreme adventure not
to be too lightly faced. In this as in other
quests he knew no distrust, but all his confidence lay in the completeness of his preparations. The sudden contrast of his frame of
mind with that recalled by the artist's placid
standard revealed a temporary disadvantage,
and he at once shrank from a premature cast of
the die. A flight across continents had at the
moment suggested a broader day, and it was to
this that Carr's words referred. Such seemed
to promise him an airing from material fumes.
From such neutral and exalted ground the right
perspective would be restored. Accordingly,
in the course of a few hours, Theodore left the
smoke of Millington behind with his face towards
the infinite.

Without following his movements in any
detail, it is enough to know that an inspiriting
flight he found it. Upon no previous occasion
had he found his mind so vigorously responsive
to the calls of the imaginative world. That

critical contest with the material seemed to have cleared the atmosphere of certain oppressive elements which had obscured his range too long. At impassioned moments Carr even felt creative might, and a whole day he spent at the ruins of Rheinfels was passed in the elaboration of a vital reminiscence in verse, beginning,

'Is mine the star which worlds have sought in vain ?'

which, however, a few days later he scattered in torn fragments to the Ischian rocks. Feeble the lines were not, but an unerring instinct assured Carr that what of the poet was his had been expended in the creation of himself. He knew no regret at the perception, for even still imaginative light shone but for him as the sun of an actual day. The supremest poetical power could never by virtue of its own have brought a ray to garret of his.

Although the man pretended to no systematic additions to his intellectual stores from so brief and erratic a journey, he was none the less conscious of considerable general advancement in that direction. Theodore had the faculty of instinctive assimilation of such material as he

knew too well he wanted. But for this it
might have seemed strange that so solitary a
man should have been able so effectually to
supply the deficiencies of the past. But the
self-educated man is built upon these self-
analyses, having unfortunately to buy his
culture at an exorbitant cost of nervous sensibility. Theodore Carr could screen these complex inner workings as successfully as most.

It was at Naples he received the impulse for
home, and he went thence direct to Marseilles.
On board the boat he made the acquaintance of
a young Englishman of literary proclivities who
(so Carr shrewdly surmised) was engaged in
the glorification of a newly-acquired bride. In
the mood in which each found himself, it
required but little intercourse to establish a
friendly footing between them, and so congenial did Theodore find this stranger's ardent
conversation that a mere suggestion was enough
to transform them for a few days into travelling
companions. Under such circumstances, it mat-
tered little to Carr that his new acquaintance
took him somewhat out of the direct path, and

so caused a slight delay in the realization of those glowing hopes upon which the whole of Theodore's mind now was bent. The delay was more than recompensed by the imaginative zest imparted by their high talk. Galbraith (such the stranger's name) was, it seemed, not bound for the inevitable Paris, but for the seclusion of the brown Brittany rocks, amongst which he meditated an indefinite stay. Inclination immediately prompted advantages in this route for Theodore also, in addition to those he would reap from the proffered company. The country they would traverse was new to him, and it would give an agreeable variation to his travels to reach home by way of the Channel Islands instead of by the ordinary route he knew so well. Thus then it was resolved.

Carr travelled with and parted from his friends in a state of characteristic fervour. The peculiar fragrance shed around them by a pair so situated was irresistible to this beholder. As his previous days had ministered mainly to his intellectual springs, so did this closing incident gild all those with its emotional rays, and speed Carr on his way in just such exalted mood as his high enterprise demanded. The noonday radiance was dazzling. Never before had Theodore approached his native land from abroad in such consummate equipment. Whatever his buoyancy, had he not previously always come to face that hard and arid path, stretching its weary length in front of the brilliant peaks to which he would attain? Whereas now at a bound he was at the verdant foot of the very peaks themselves. Small wonder if his heart was stout.

Despite previous intentions, the traveller found himself unable to linger on his way. He reached St. Helier's one afternoon, and took passage for Southampton the morning following. Even the weather could not deter him. The billows of cloud and sea rather stimulated his vigorous mood, and he gave himself up to the mercies of the deep in a vein of wild hilarity.

Nor were his spirits damped by the coolness of his reception. Under a leaden sky and all the discomforts of south-west torrents, he landed late in the afternoon, and was glad to escape from the hands of the Custom House officials to the train which was waiting to convey him on his homeward flight. He was to proceed directly to London, and thence take the night train to Millington,—the urgency of his impulsive movements not permitting any more delay.

It was with a peculiar sense of satisfaction that Theodore lighted his cigar. With half closed eyes he beheld the sordid world about him through a haze of rosy tolerance. Of such he scarcely now felt himself to form a part. Throughout this tour he had adjusted his mode of travelling to the altered conditions of his purse, and the result had been gratifying. Past benevolence had by no means faded from his mind. His heart positively glowed with charitable warmth to all mankind. If he spent lavishly upon himself, he gave alms upon a still more extravagant scale when opportunity offered. Nothing but purely temporary tactics of his own stood between him and a munificent scheme for the amelioration of at any rate a definite section of pastoral life. He might even have urged that these apparently selfish steps were absolutely essential to his benevolent plan, and a logical introduction to that long-projected enterprise. Memory carried Theodore back to the green shelter of the Swinging Tree. Had it not been pronounced by lips which carried all the weight of irrevocable law to him?

The train stopped, and Carr looked slumberously out upon the lights. He had been dozing, and perhaps faces had presented themselves to him in those half-conscious visions upon which his soul could dwell with calm delight. At any rate, a placid serenity lay upon his refined and handsome features as he turned them to the window at his side, and he doubtless afforded a subject of impatient and curious contemplation to hurrying passengers that caught a glimpse of him from without. There were not many such, but his eyes responded to those that passed with unruffled kindliness. Whilst thus engaged, a sudden change came over him, and he leaped up from his seat, as it seemed, in a spasm of alarm.

There was nothing immediately to explain

such unexpected movement. If Carr's eyes were followed in their startled gaze, they were seen but to rest upon two inoffensive passengers standing in conversation by the door of the refreshment-room. The features of one of them certainly were noticeable for their animation and (being a woman) striking charm. But general sensibility was by no means the emotion which Theodore betrayed. As the train just moved, he threw down the window, and seemed upon the point of getting out, but an official checked him. Carr acquiesced, but, disregarding the man, kept his eyes fixed upon that particular spot. Both of those faces turned to watch the train depart, but paid no especial heed to the part where Theodore was. Their movement seemed, however, to give him some assurance of which his anxious stare had stood in need, and in pale nervous wakefulness he sank again into his seat.

He did not doze again.

CHAPTER XII.

DIVINITY TESTED.

CALM reason could not sustain the ridiculous fears with which Carr had been so unaccountably overwhelmed. Having crossed London, and being once again ensconced in an easy corner, whirling along towards all that his life had held most dear, he even smiled complacently at the vague shadow which had caused the pang. True, reason with all its powerful light could not dispel the fact that it was Laura Blakenhurst whom he had seen; did not suggest any evasion of it. But were there not a hundred explanations of her presence there? Because his mind held her inseparably associated with a certain spot, was she to be restricted to the bounds of that imaginative limit? He regained a more reasonable attitude.

Still it seemed probable that he must submit at least to a temporary disappointment. None the less, when at home, he wrote in the small hours of the night an announcement of his return to Mr. Lindred. Impetuosity demanded so much. The next morning it was posted, and Carr had not long to wait for the coveted answer.

'Come, by all means at any time,' the artist wrote.

Theodore sent an appointment for the following Monday.

There were four days to elapse before that— a concession probably to Carr's new hopes rather than to any spirit of politeness. It afforded at least just a bare possibility of Laura's return, and she away, Theodore would this time have felt a visit to Winwold depressing and vain. Short as it was, he had some difficulty in spanning the interval. To his chagrin Carr found that, continental exhilaration notwithstanding, the very atmosphere of Millington affected him adversely. If he walked through the streets he was seized with a spirit of dejection. It was a general rather than specific impression. Even to himself Carr admitted no determinate cause. If he met an acquaintance he felt a shock of irritation. He hated to be seen abroad. Not even to his friend, the curator, did he feel genially inclined. He wanted to be alone, or better still amongst a crowd to which he was utterly unknown. So imperative did this become that on the Saturday he went to Birmingham to obtain the respite he required, intending to stay there until his departure for Winwold early on Monday.

The change at first afforded him the desired effect. All his buoyancy returned, and with it the rosy aspect of the world. An inordinate liberality always accompanied this condition in him, and as Carr prowled about the streets that Saturday night, he stealthily thrust shillings into unsuspecting hands, the astonished recipients turning in vain to catch a glimpse of their mysterious benefactor. He commenced this mainly in sport, but as he found it a stimulating diversion, he went to it at length with systematic ardour. He would change gold into as many shillings as he could conveniently carry, and then scatter amazement throughout the crowded highways. Such was Carr's method of dissipation from which he did not retire until the small hours.

He dreamed vividly in the night, and when he woke in the morning to the unmusical tone of a church bell, Theodore lay for some time in but a half-conscious state of reverie. The scenes of the night before flitted again across his imagination, but with a subtle significance of suggestion which had not been presented to his waking sight. The appalling reality of that spectacle of wretchedness was irresistibly borne in upon him, and seemed suddenly to connect itself with some far-away sensations which he scarcely knew to have been his own. The gloom and bitterness of the world oppressed a soul over which only its sweetness and light had hitherto much prevailed. Carr would willingly have assured himself that he was dreaming still, had not the wish but too vehemently gainsaid its object. Just as he was again sinking into an actual doze, features which he knew, from amidst that ghastly throng, pierced him with a glance of intolerable pathos, and at the sound of an imaginary voice he leaped up.

There was somebody at the door with his shaving-water.

From this sinister commencement uneasy thoughts clung about Carr of which even the broad daylight of the town could not at once relieve him. Empty though the streets were, or at most sprinkled with well-dressed citizens of orderly intent, to one gaze they were still peopled with crowded woe. If only as a refuge from this disordered state, Theodore went into a church to which he came, the clock of which announced the hour of prayer. He took a seat by the door, and before the service was over he came out, rendered impatient by some incongruity which had struck him there. But none the less he had gained some of that composure he had sought.

He paid no particular heed to his steps as he left the church. One way led at a few paces to the broad thoroughfare of the world, the other to still deeper and duskier by-ways. Carr had taken the latter.

Before going far, he became aware of being an object of scrutiny to two dirty children that he had casually noticed there, who seemed of the crop indigenous to pavements. Now they were shuffling along the other side of the way, evidently intent upon some estimate of the imposing stranger. As Carr turned to look at them, the little boy touched his forehead (cap he had none) and seemed inclined to cross the street. Blind factory-walls were on either side, a fact which perhaps induced Carr to stop. The children came to him and muttered the customary plea for a copper.

Theodore was not in the mood to fling them one and pass on. He questioned the boy who was the spokesman, and got, as he thought with equivocal fluency, the customary tale of squalor and privation.

'Will you take me home?' said Carr, rather severely.

'Father's doing fourteen days, sir; mother 'll be drunk,' was the boy's reply.

'Never mind—let me see.'

To Carr's astonishment, the boy readily acquiesced, and set off to lead the way.

A silence fell upon Carr as he followed his odd guides, and he was so absorbed in his own subjects of contemplation that he did not observe the sly glances which were cast upon him from time to time. They turned into one foul alley after another, making a circuitous rather than a progressive route, had Carr been observant enough to detect it, until all at once even the philanthropic sense became alarmed. Theodore looked about to severely question his little leaders only to see that they were gone. Stare this way and that as he would, no vestige of them remained, no indication of the manner of their flight. Carr's uneasiness was naturally heightened under the suspicion that he had been taken in a trap. But there was nothing else to sustain his alarm. No ruffians appeared, and there seemed little difficulty in effecting an escape. It was a squalid enough street to be sure, but open to the sky, and, as it seemed, of interminable length. Some children played on the curbstone, and in the dingy doorways some women talked, but to this stranger and his affairs nobody seemed to pay any particular regard. Carr could only suppose it a humorous freak on the part of the disappointed urchins, who meant to have out, in pure mischief, the value of the copper denied them in coin.

Such was his decision, and he was in the act of hastening away when suddenly the same boy was again at his feet. This time he was alone.

'Mother ain't drunk, sir,' he said, before Carr could speak. 'Will you come and see?'

'No, you can give her this,'—and the philanthropist thrust a shilling into the child's hand. The latter simply stared in astonishment, and, as Carr thought, looked for the instant honest. 'Yes, I will come,' added he, as an afterthought. 'Which is the house?'

The boy took him a few paces back, and then turned up a narrow arched passage. Theodore followed this time, ashamed of his fears. Had not some such quarter once been *home* to him also ? With a shudder at the thought, he entered the dingy court, paved so as to slant to a drain in the centre, and across which stretched a line whereon sundry 'washing' was hung. After he had bowed beneath the rags to reach the door to which the boy was leading, Carr's eyes encountered those of another figure—a strange one for such locality—which issued from a doorway just beyond.

'This is it, sir.'

Carr turned mechanically to the boy, but then abruptly looked round again. Nobody was there. The apparition had gone. The child's eyes were riveted in wonderment upon his mysterious friend's face, so striking was the change in him.

'Who was that?' asked Carr.

'District visitor, sir, I think they call 'em.'

'But don't you know her name ? Which door did she go into ? Does she often come here?'

A woman came from within the doorway by which they were standing, and cringed to Carr. He merely stared at her.

'I don't think that lady has been before, sir ?'

'No, no, it must be my mistake,' smiled Carr; and, taking from his pocket what seemed to be a handful of silver, he gave it to the woman and fled.

Carr could not command his thoughts until he had taken several aimless turnings, then he went back. For upwards of an hour he vainly wandered in search of that dingy archway, of the boy that led him thither, of the spirit that he there had seen; but it was to no purpose. When he at length found himself before the church which he had originally left, he seemed to acknowledge his defeat, for he walked slowly along the way which he knew to lead into the lighter world. The main streets now presented a very different appearance, for the population had risen, and as it was a fine day the pavement was beginning to assume its aspect of afternoon promenade. Carr hurried to his hotel, and he did not again go forth for the remainder of the day.

Despite his extraordinary efforts, therefore, Theodore was not to present himself at Win-wold in any superabundant spirits. An uneasy suspicion that the world was not to be that very plain and intelligible matter which to his eager sense it had hitherto appeared could not be altogether extinguished. It is true that as the sullen grey atmosphere which crowned the housetops was left for the free expanse of heaven over the meadows, shadowed by finely clustered storm-clouds glorious in their frowning, much of the weight was blown from Carr's mind, and he began to discern in clearer outline the goal whither he was bound, and the pleasant path whereby he was to reach it. After all, the unwonted uncertainty of his spirits caused him less surprise when in this country air he regathered the conviction that he was in love. With his feet upon the grass, only Laura had power over him,—a power which was exercised only for the highest purposes which man can know, and for buckling on the weapons whereby such purposes were to be finally attained. He began again to perceive this, and therefore consciously to assert it by way of preparation for the fray. It reconciled much. Nay, it suffused all with a brilliance and warmth of human emotion without which life would appeal little to Theodore Carr. How much that startling and distracting vision in Birmingham squalor might mean, he did not pretend as yet to decide, but from this distance he was able to see that it contained nothing from which he need shrink. The possibilities rather were that a germ of universal reconciliation for the contending elements of subterranean Carr lay therein. The fulness of this thought only occurred to him as the train stopped at Gosstall, the station for Winwold, else doubtless he would more thoroughly have worked it; but as it was it afforded him an inspiriting subject of contemplation for his drive across the downs.

Theodore did not disguise the importance of the high enterprise upon which he was bent. Save for that accidental encounter in the quarry several years ago, he had never spoken to Laura; yet had long musing upon her, assiduous gathering of all possible evidence concerning her, and, above all, instinctive interpretation of the exquisite features which had so deeply impressed him, inspired him with a confident knowledge of her character. In the appropriation of so much excellence to his own exclusive use he had never known an instant's discouragement. He had a strong conviction that it was ordained of the fates; a conviction which had no doubt assisted him to his peculiarly delicate method of pursuit. Laura was now nearing twenty, and to the eye a very mature and lovely woman: Carr pronounced his own equipment adequate, therefore they might meet. The powers had opportunely planted the artist Lindred at Winwold for this one particular purpose. Having met, Theodore pronounced it wholly within his power as to what the result should be. Heaven be his speed!

Mr. Lindred greeted him warmly, and the short time which had to elapse before the hour of luncheon was passed in the green shade of the orchard. The congenial personal contact at once aroused Carr's vivacity, and he was able to merge in more general interests the absorbing purpose which he had so lately acknowledged as his only object here. The interpretation of the 'Fair Enigma' had of course been but a polite apology on the artist's part for extending a friendly invitation to one so little known, and he by no means regarded Carr through the medium of a mysterious young woman merely. He had instinctively formed a high estimate of Carr's intelligence and character, and in face of that he had an inexhaustible supply of interesting topics.

Still at intervals, as the day advanced, Theodore was doomed to be conscious that he was acting a part, and, when at last all had separated for the night, he felt definite surprise at the fact that the enigma had not once even jocularly been referred to. He did not sleep well, partly through a too active fancy, partly through the hooting of the owls.

Early in the morning Carr went out, as was invariably his custom in the country. Natural effects always exhilarated him keenly, and he found no disappointment to-day. The subtle influence of this particular locality had lost none of its power. It was not a brilliant morning, but to Carr suggestive enough. Belonging neither to summer nor autumn, it partook of

the character of both. A cold white mist overspread the valley, and over the grass you could
see the cows' and the labourers' tracks through
the frost-like dew. From the sky, pale-blue
and cloudless, the sun peered dimly over the
eastern hill with just sufficient strength to throw
an indeterminate shadow. Chiff-chaffs still piped
from the hedge, and at the roots of the thick
brambles blackbirds were raking and chuck-
ling. There was no wind, but when Carr reached
the top of the ridge a cool breath from the
north-east fanned his face, and the sound of the
trains some miles away seemed to be at a field
or two's distance from him. Here he stood for
some minutes to listen and muse upon the
sound. Presently it ceased, then suddenly was
clear again, and Carr knew that the train had
passed the tunnel. A woodpecker flung a detached note; a single rook cawed in passing;
and then a heavy, shuffling footstep on the road
interrupted the man's reverie. Turning round,
Carr saw that countryman of his acquaintance,
Thomas Warrilow,—the man who had first enlightened him about Saloway, and with whom

upon his several visits he generally exchanged an amicable word. They passed the day to each other, and Carr's attitude encouraged Warrilow to stop.

'Good air here, sir, quite,' remarked he, looking about him.

'So good that I think of coming to live here,' replied Carr, good-humouredly.

'Do you, sir? Well, we'll be glad to see you, however. Old times be greatly changed, more's the pity. Them as be up in the world have no correspondence with we, and it be my opinion as it do harm to both.'

'I think so . . . Why do you think that I should be different?'

'You'll excuse my speech, sir,' said the man, with deference. 'No disrespect to anybody, very far from it, but one can't help but notice things. Our squire (and Mr. Vivian an' all, for that,) never had no respect for their fellow-man, do what 'em would.'

'I suppose not,' remarked Carr, absently. 'But—but Miss Laura is different.'

'That her were, but who'd ha' had a notion

of this start, at last?' said the countryman, in an undertone, and with one of those arch, upward glances meant to imply so much.

This instantly recalled Carr, and he looked into the man's face.

'You'll have heard about it, sir, I count?'

All Carr's sickening and vague depression of recent days was gathered into that one clouded second during which he stared again at his companion, and said,

'About what?'

Before the reply was uttered, he felt the heavens had closed over him.

'Why, her've married Tom Chatwin, and gone into foreign parts. 'Em do say as her be a-married, however, but 'twould be hazardous to say which way.'

'And who is Tom Chatwin?' said Carr, with a composure which under the circumstances was tragical.

'Master Chatwin's son o' the Knapp. A common labouring man a were,—the father, however,—and the son be'nt much better. No scholar for the like o' she. 'Em tell me as the squire be like to lose his intellects over the concern, for a thought a deal o' Miss Laura.'

'H'm, quite a village romance,' remarked Theodore, looking to the horizon. 'Some of you ought to make a ballad about it.'

'Well, well,' laughed Warrilow, at what he considered an admirable joke.

'But when did this happen?'

'Last Monday I was a-talking to Miss Laura as it might be to you, sir, at this minute, and it do appear as on Wednesday morning Mr. Vivian got a letter to say that 'em were wed. There is a common report as he followed 'em to Southampton, and had a fight with Tom in the street, but Mr. Vivian be'nt much of a hand, so I doubt, as we say in our plain Gloucestershire way, common report be a liar in this respect. He came home a Saturday night, however, and there have been strange doings up at the Hall, by all accounts.'

'There must have been,' said Carr, and muttering an adieu, he took out his watch and turned away rather abruptly.

How much of this remarkable story was

worthy of belief, Theodore was not in a condition just now to determine. That something tragical and conclusive had come over the hopes of his existence his instinct at once knew, and as the tutored soul receives really critical strokes, he accepted it with unfathomed calmness.

He found Dorothy in the garden cutting the blossom which was to be laid at each place at the table,—a pretty custom of hers whether with or without visitors,—and she was aware of no change in him. They went in together, talking, and greeted the artist in the breakfast-room where he was reading the newspaper—the previous day's, come by post.

'H'm—sad,' said he, and lowered the paper to take Carr's hand. They exchanged a few words on the visitor's morning observations.

Dorothy, who had done at the table, asked her father what was sad.

'Only one of those tourist accidents,' replied he, giving the paper to her; 'on the Brittany rocks.—That is the normal effect of the east here,' he went on again facing Carr. 'As to the sounds, you have to remember that in a mist they travel with especial clearness——'

Breakfast was served, and they took their places.

Carr had so far managed to sustain his part well, but when it came to eating, the trial was severe.   It seemed physically impossible for him to swallow his food.   He tried to talk vivaciously in order to disguise the cause of his indifferent appetite.   In the artificial enthusiasm to which this at last raised him, he managed to take the plunge before which his soul had been shivering.

'By-the-by,' said he, 'this is a singular story about your squire's daughter.'

The artist's eyes turned rather suddenly upon the speaker, but Carr's placid smile was ready for the gaze.

'More light on the enigma,' Mr. Lindred said. 'How did you hear of it?'

'What, she is the enigma!—A rustic gossip gave me some picturesque outlines up the hill this morning.'

It seemed both to Dorothy and her father that

this was a singularly cynical tone for one who had spoken so ardently in the studio a month or two ago.

'Is it true that she has married this squire of low degree?'

'Quite true,' said the artist, going on with his meal and not disguising his disinclination for the talk. 'They have gone to the Cape, I understand.—But it is an appalling tragedy.'

There was something in the artist's voice which Theodore had not before heard and which, finding an echo in the depths of his own being, struck him dumb. None of them quite succeeded in dispelling the cloud for the rest of the time at table.

Carr had an uneasy impression that, in his effort to act the worldly part, he had appeared unfavourably before his friends. Since it had been at the cost also of his own most sacred feelings, he was not long in deciding to throw off the mask; so far, that is, as such candour was consistent with merely a general display. On rising from the table, Mr. Lindred had invited him to the studio, so without scruple Carr made his appearance there.

'May I see the picture again?' he said at once; and, without hesitation, the artist placed his portrait of Laura where Dorothy had put it before.

'You have altered it!' exclaimed Carr, abruptly.

'Do you disapprove?'

'Most vehemently.'

'In the face of recent development?'

'There is possibility—certainty, of crime now, and it is unnatural to such a face.'

'I had hoped so more ardently than yourself,' was Lindred's response, 'but the harsh truth has subdued me.'

'But what evil has she done—can she possibly do?—You are mistaken.'

'Womanhood is our only ideal possession. In the highest it dwells absolutely inviolable.'

'But may not excess of highest womanhood impel to its own apparent violation?'

'By no manner of means,' declared the artist, his marvellously calm deep eyes fixed upon Carr, with whose manner and appearance he was now vastly more satisfied.

'But is not love beyond the reach of conventional proprieties?'

'Conventional proprieties, yes; but to a rational life it is on the other hand the essential key. Tamper with that, and human existence becomes a devil's farce.

> "If you loved only what were worth your love,
> Love were clear gain, and wholly well for you."

All centres in it, and herein the germ of womanhood lies. *The* woman cannot love unworthily.'

'And has our enigma, then? You, I know, cannot regard the mere social glove. I know nothing of the man.'

'I do not regard the social glove, as you remark, (although, by the way, excellence is mighty apocryphal without it,) but this man is worthless exactly in proportion to your philosophical analysis of him.'

'Then perhaps she did not love him.'

'How so?'

'Might there not be some other motive for the step?'

Lindred's amazement disconcerted Carr, and,

under the impression that he was construed as heaping still more dishonour upon Laura's head, Theodore lost the thought which had flashed over him, and he regarded the picture in silent despair.

'No, no, my friend, we cannot mend matters, so let us accept them with a sigh, and forget that human nature has once again given us a slip.'

All power of argument was dead in Carr, although his whole soul rose in rebellion against this base verdict upon the vision whereon all his recent life was built.

'You will dispose of that picture?' was all he said, with an attempted smile.

'Impossible. It interests me extremely.'

'Then you will do one for me?'

'I cannot promise it.'

The artist was removing the canvas, and, having been placed away in its corner, it was not again referred to during the remainder of Carr's visit.

There were two more days to be surmounted, no light task in view of the effect of this beginning upon the visitor. Despite the most heroic efforts, Theodore knew himself to be the most intolerable company, and urged various excuses for shortcomings which others could not see. It is true that it could be easily perceived that he was not especially brilliant, that he frequently appeared preoccupied; but the artist, knowing of the revolution in Carr's commercial and pecuniary affairs (and having, moreover, learnt something of his previous history) was astonished rather at the amount of self-confidence he was able to display.

One or two of the new magazines were of assistance, and in the evening, as Carr chanced to be looking at one, he came across a page of verses signed 'Owen Galbraith.' He thought them good, and drew Dorothy's attention to them.

'Odd,' said he; 'that is a man I met recently in the Mediterranean. I crossed France with him, and left him in Brittany.'

'With his wife?' added Dorothy, looking up.

'Certainly. How did you know? Do you know him?'

Dorothy did not, but she recalled the fact that such was the name mentioned in the newspaper account of the accident in Brittany the day before. Carr evinced genuine interest and concern, and the newspaper was looked out for his perusal. There could be small doubt of the identity, and Theodore read with peculiarly sympathetic horror that that brilliant, newly-acquired wife was killed. It haunted him throughout the evening, and, as they were parting at bed-time, he announced his determination to leave early in the morning for Brittany.

Possibly the definite cause of action prompted him as strongly as his wounded sensibility. Perhaps the comparison of his own calamity with that suffered by one to whom he had felt powerfully drawn, prompted a desire for the society of that other. In the morning, at any rate, Carr set off.

He was in Brittany the following day, only to hear that Galbraith had buried his wife and gone. His disappointment was extreme . . . Whither? . . . 'A Londres.' . . . Nothing more

precise could be obtained. However, to London Carr accordingly pursued ; but, by the time
he set foot in the Strand, a change had come
over himself, and he no longer felt impelled to
discover his afflicted fellow-traveller.

For the first time for many years the depressed,
and to some extent disillusioned, man found, of
all places, the dingy streets of Millington the
refuge which his soul required. Thither he
went that day.

CHAPTER XIII.

BACK-WATER.

MR. LINDRED succumbed to Carr's importunity, and a replica of the 'Fair Enigma' at length adorned the young timber-merchant's wall. There it acquired much of the significance of a shrine to him.

The extraordinary action of Miss Laura Blakenhurst naturally excited much comment. So remote from philosophic or imaginative impulse is the common mind, that her step was unintelligible, save by way of vulgar irregularity of the tender passion. This, when directed to any social discomfiture, is traditionally a crime in woman; as a crime it was generally imputed to Laura in consequence.

In view of a prolonged transcendental estimate of her, such explanation was, as we have seen, not sufficient for Carr. Crime in her was for ever impossible, as thunder from a cloudless sky, therefore must some other way be found.

With this purpose did Theodore devote hours of his days to the exhaustive interpretation of the enigma; a task sweet though embittering, and one to which he went with irresistible ardour whatever the anguish hidden in it for himself. Whatever his conclusion of the matter, certain it was that as a personal aspiration Laura was dead to him, and never until now had he really recognised what a vital source of all his own later effort she had become. At moments it seemed to him that his very life itself had been involved in this chimerical adventure, and that, the crown extinguished, there was no further call for breath. Confused visions of a shattered, wholly frustrate existence assailed him, into which crept gloomy suggestions of the relative merits of the motives whereupon his life had been built. In so unnerved a condition, sensitive hints, which had hitherto been easily and magnanimously disposed of, assumed the shape of disquieting scruples from which there was no escape. So tyrannical did these shades become, that at length in sheer self-defence Carr plunged again into commercial engagements.

From them, however, he was not to draw any lasting balm. The uncompromising quality of his instincts denied him practical refuge of this kind. From sensual pleasures, moreover, he found that he now recoiled, and from all sources of refined enjoyment he was debarred by the insidious glances which lurked within them. Thus it was that irresistibly, from day to day, Carr was thrust further and further towards that vision which had affected him so powerfully, and withal so irreconcilably, in the Birmingham by-ways.

So essential is self-deception to a certain temperament, that even yet Theodore confronted that but vaguely. Never had the resolution to find and munificently recompense Saloway and Emily for a moment faded from his mind. With Laura it was to be undertaken by way of crowning celebration of his union with her. Laura's opinion of her father's behaviour to the revolutionary cobbler he had heard from her own lips, there had always seemed therefore an alluring artistic fitness in his being the agent for redeeming the Blakenhurst family from so gross an imputation, and at the same time restoring poor Saloway to the rights of life. Circumstances had inevitably affected this motive, and perhaps the tardiness with which he approached the narrow road bespoke a grain of ungraciousness in his impulse.

Like a schoolboy who has long toiled over his task unsuccessfully, one morning Carr awoke to find his enigma solved. It might almost seem that he had dreamed it, for the full clear thought possessed him wholly with his earliest consciousness. Laura had sacrificed herself. Not in the pursuit of her own selfish, impetuous needs had she flung the world away, as her grosser critics imputed; but deliberately, as a conscious oblation. He himself had heard her speak of a crusade, though her father should be the Saracen; this she had found impracticable, therefore had she carried her warfare higher against the very nature of things itself. To his clear morning vision this was all-sufficing, and, as an instinctive corollary, Carr found light also for himself. What *she* had done might not *he* do also? For that day the thought haunted and allured him. In the evening he took train to Birmingham.

As he alighted upon the platform, he almost collided with a man who had issued from the adjoining compartment.

'I thought it was you,' said the stranger, by way of apology, and, looking up, Carr was astonished by the face of his Mediterranean acquaintance Galbraith, whom he had so vainly sought. That was a month ago, yet was there something incongruous to Theodore's mind still in the contented, almost jocular appearance of the afflicted poet. Nevertheless, Carr took the hand and pressed it sympathetically, without any reference to the circumstances of their previous meeting, or his own impulsive pursuit.

They stood back to have the necessary preliminary conversation after both had acknowledged that they were not travelling farther.

In the course of their talk, Galbraith confessed a journalistic object in his visit; had a paper to do on one of the midland industries; he was going to a hotel. No pressure was necessary to get him to accompany Carr as a guest at any rate for dinner, and off they went.

The man of letters was pre-eminently sociable, although when Carr came to examine him more closely in a bright light he discerned traces of the shock he had sustained. Galbraith looked noticeably older, cast harsher looks upon the world, threw out cynical retorts from time to time, and moreover had absent moments, when the observant Carr detected an undercurrent which he deemed the habitual vivacity was assumed to hide. Under the companionship, Theodore's own spirits began to rise.

Three days was Galbraith to stay. On the evening of the second, when he came to dinner, instead of finding Carr awaiting him, as had been agreed, a note was there to explain that his friend had been called away on business, and, it was much to be feared, would not be able to see him again before his return to

London; but would Galbraith (Carr added) send his town address to Millington, so that they might meet up there when there was occasion fitting.

Presumably, therefore, Theodore had once more returned to Millington, but such was not actually the case. The exhilaration with which Galbraith's society threatened Carr's sombre instincts had awakened scruples whereby he had been spurred to definite action. He had felt that once more an ignoble temptation was assailing him just at the moment that he had succeeded in discovering the right path, and momentary vigour enabled him to withstand the assault.

After writing the explanatory note for Galbraith, Carr had left the hotel as twilight was falling, and made his way rather hurriedly to the neighbourhood of the market. After looking through one or two of the dingy streets about there, he found what he sought, and entered it. This was an old clothes' shop, which proved to be insufferably redolent of coarse leather and fustian. The fat woman came forward with deference, and Theodore visibly shrank before her panting urbanity.

'I want some clothes for a working printer,' began Carr, in a patronising manner, as he cast his eyes over the various garments suspended around him. 'The poor fellow has nothing whatever to come in, so——'

'Oh, we can fit him, sir—'ph—'ph—is he a big man?'

'About my own size, I should think; but no doubt you would change any article which—'

'With pleasure, sir. I always tries to accommodate my customers, more partiklerly the poor.'

Not being willing to refine the excruciating torture which he had voluntarily elected to undergo, Carr made no further comment, but in grim silence inspected the articles recommended, and in a very few minutes decided upon a suit which would answer his benevolent purpose.

'Any boots, sir?'

Yes, boots were necessary.

'A hat?'

Carr shuddered. No, at a hat he drew the

line.   He thought the object of his bounty had
one.   For the present this would do.   In the
face of detailed persuasion Theodore grew
wroth, and the woman recognized the limit.
But as the price asked and obtained covered a
large transaction of an ordinary kind, she was
well content.   With a large brown paper parcel
Carr escaped from the suffocating shop, and at
the end of the street paused to consider his
purpose.

'Ay,' soliloquised the fortunate woman in the
meantime, as she again regarded her coin, 'if
there were a few more o' they practical pherlan-
thopists, what a word'ld it would be, to be
sure !'

As a man came along lighting the lamps, Carr
moved onwards, and in a minute or two he
plunged into a disreputable public-house, over
the door of which in the glass of a dark red
lamp he had read the sign, 'The Shades.'   No
Theodore Carr came thence again, but after a
short space of time a decent young artisan in
his Sunday clothes was hurrying from this street
as though fearing detection in so discreditable

a quarter. A man of ragged and vicious appearance followed him to the corner at a heavy shuffling trot, but as a coin glistened in the lamplight and jingled on the stones, the ruffian snorted and stopped short, whilst the youth had at a run effected his escape, not slackening his pace until he felt pursuit impossible.

By dint of inquiry, this young man found his way to a certain church which was at no great distance from the low quarter whence we have seen him issue. At the angle of two streets opposite the main gateway of the church, lights displayed a small newsvendor's window to which the man drew. He glanced at the bills and paper literature exposed there, then moved away. After slowly pacing the pavement surrounding the church, he came again to this shop window, and as a child was coming out of the doorway he looked inside. The next moment he also entered.

'I see you have some lodgings to let,' he said to the man who was reading at the counter. 'May I see them?'

A scrutinizing stare was his first reception, but as though ashamed of so blunt a betrayal of his suspicions, the shopkeeper dropped his eyes, and said, 'Certainly,' adding that it was but one room furnished plainly as a bed-room.

The housewife of the establishment was called, and the inspection made.

Civil, middle-aged people these seemed to be upon a closer examination, and, upon the visitor expressing satisfaction with the accommodation and the terms, there was even a suspicion of delicacy in the woman's mode of eliciting personal details of her prospective lodger. The latter on his part met her frankly, and announced himself one Thomas Clarke, a timber-merchant's clerk, out of employment just then, but with sufficient funds for some weeks, and prepared to pay every week in advance. The man's behaviour was re-assuring and his proposal sound, so that the agreement was concluded there and then.

The newsvendor proved to be a man of some originality of character, and from the outset evinced a strong partiality for his lodger. After a few days' tentative experience of each other, Clarke boarded wholly with the family, (the man and his wife, that is; there were no children,) and he was given clearly to understand that his company after closing hours was more than acceptable downstairs. If for no other reason, the dogmatic shopkeeper willingly accepted so intelligent a pair of ears whereinto to pour all the zeal and eloquence of his social and political cranks. The man's central fanaticism was, the land for the people and the people on the land, and nightly would he pursue this topic into all its fiery ramifications through what he emphatically called 'the stinking miasma of a pestilential slough' (pronounced sloff) 'of landlordism and robbery.'

But Clarke evidently was not prepared to enter deeply into his friend's ardent speculations. He listened admirably, and frankly admitted agreement upon theoretical points, but was in no mood to take part in active propagandism. He even declined to accompany the shopkeeper to meetings of enthusiasts at an adjoining tavern, held every Saturday night, where these particular tenets were exhaustively discussed. Indeed, despite the obvious congeniality so soon established, the newsvendor and his wife were not long in discerning something mysterious in the personality of their lodger. The woman hinted to her husband religious mania, for she asserted that he had attended every service at the church opposite, week-days though they were, that had been celebrated since his arrival. Her explanation, however, received some discredit when the second Sunday morning came, and Clarke did not go out before the bells had stopped. He had gone up to his room presumably to prepare for church, but had not come down again. This was so unexpected that the landlady easily found occasion for some domestic office upstairs.

Clarke was sitting at his window when the woman knocked, entered, apologized, and withdrew, just as he had been doing since the commencement of the church bells. Her movement received no notice from him, and he said nothing to her apology. His eyes remained fixed upon the iron gateway through which some time ago the last worshipper had entered, and his face was unusually pale, even haggard. He was still sitting there, more than an hour later, when some children came running from the door in advance of the general congregation. But then he suddenly seized his hat, and went out.

As though suspecting the eyes of his inquisitive landlady, Clarke put the church between him and his dwelling before taking up a position on the pavement to the south. By skilful management he could command therefrom* a tolerably full view of all issuing from the church doorway, even should they turn abruptly round towards the north side of the church. He had stood there but a few seconds when a deep colour suffused the whole of his clean-shaven features, and he altered his position. After looking intently in a certain direction, he darted across to a narrow street opposite and ran, turning again at the first corner to the right. One more turn brought him to a broader thoroughfare along which were coming several passengers. He threw his eyes eagerly along the pavement, and then turned round and lingered. After several of the people he had noticed had passed the end of his narrow by-way, he also advanced and walked boldly into the wider street.

His pace, his movements, and the activity of his eyes now at once showed that his object was to keep certain figures in view, without himself incurring the risk of observation. Owing to the number before him, it could not be immediately determined which individual was the object of his scrutiny. When presently, however, he turned off into a less frequented street, the task was easier. From end to end of this street there were only visible a man and a young woman with their backs in Clarke's direction, and a girl coming on the other side towards him. When the latter had passed, he crossed over to her side, and still went forward.

It was, then, with the movements of the other pair that he was engaged. His eyes now were not permitted to leave them for an instant, although the distance at which he followed was to some extent increased.

The street was a long, straight one, changing much in quality as it ascended a slope. The houses were smaller, and from being buildings of a mercantile appearance became artisan dwellings with a small shop-window here and there. It was in this part that those two figures stopped. Clarke watched them mount the two steps in front of a door which he marked intently, and, as soon as they had entered, he went to that side of the street and walked quickly forward. On the door as he passed it he read the number 159, and glancing at the window by its side— the ordinary parlour-window of such a house, with the blind drawn down—he saw at the bottom corner, by the grace of the irregularity of the blind, a portion of a workman's boot. With this glimpse Clarke passed on, and made his way back to his lodging by another route.

The following morning Clarke told his land-lady that, as he had not succeeded in finding work, he should have to resume his travels once more. The announcement was received with astonishment and frank regret,—even the news-vendor's magniloquent advice was unavailing,—and Clarke took his leave.

He went direct to Primrose Hill, the street wherein his pursuit had ended the previous day, and in the broad daylight applied for lodgings at three or four of the houses opposite to No. 159. At length at No. 80 he succeeded.

'I shall always pay in advance,' he said to the woman with whom he was dealing, and laying the sum demanded for the first week on the table as he spoke. 'I have to move about a good deal,' added he, 'and may be absent sometimes for some days at a time, but of course that will not affect the payment. I shall want my room to be kept whether I am here or not. In fact, I shall be away to-night.'

'Exactly. I had a brother as was a com-mission agent myself,' said the woman, 'so I know what it is.'

'Certainly.'

Mr. Carr had not been to his timber-office for

some days, but it chanced that he appeared there that evening shortly before the time of closing.

CHAPTER XIV.

FROM NO. 159.

'You do too much at it, maidie,' said Benjamin Saloway to his daughter, as they sat at dinner, for which Emily showed but scant appetite. 'Charity be a good thing, we all know, but I can't think as we were ever meant to do injury to ourselves along of it. My father 'd used to talk of old Parson Harrison of Upton, as how he was always there in the day of trial and treated the poor in the best o' ways at all times, but none the less as he kept a tall, stout man to the last, and a was eighty-five when a died.'

'I am sure I can believe it, father,' replied Emily, with a smile. 'There is nothing so good for the health as active charity, and it is certainly not that which hurts me. I have not got such a strong body as Parson Harrison, that's all. You may be sure that, if I did not do *my* poor work of charity, I should not be so well as I am.'

'Well, well, Emily, you be a queer 'un, I always say.'

And silence once more settled upon them.

It was a Sunday morning, and Emily had returned home, as it seemed, more than usually exhausted. As a rule, she accompanied her father to the church of their adoption, but this particular day she had instead been sitting with a sick woman in a squalid court of this more or less particularly squalid parish. On this occasion the young woman spoke literal truth to her father. It was not her charitable labour which affected her appetite and blanched her cheeks. That morning Emily had had a singular and a startling experience, for her eyes had tried to make her believe that once more she had beheld Theodore Carr, and under circumstances in themselves astounding.

This glimpse, dream, vision, or whatever it was, had had an extraordinary effect upon Emily, and she could not in any case have disclosed to her father the real cause of her disquiet. For one thing, the peculiar quality of the emotion aroused in her was of an unspeakable nature, had there not been other forcible impulses to reticence. Since their flight of more than four years ago, in conversation the name of Theodore Carr had not escaped the lips either of father or daughter.

This, of course, was but small indication of the tenor of their thoughts, for it would not be rash to assert that no day had passed in those years which had escaped them whereof the name of Theodore Carr did not form for both an essential part. The 'he will find us' which had confessedly sustained Emily through the first tragic weeks after their clouded exodus had inevitably become merged in another syllabled burden as these weeks had drawn themselves out to months, and these months again to years. Had elemental question and answer been possible with Emily, as

she was leaving her home early that Sunday
morning, she would doubtless have confessed
that that brilliant companion of her sunlit girl-
hood had at last sunk into as immaterial a
dream for her as any sinking rays of the sun
itself which she had gazed on during the same
period.   It was the sudden desertion of this
unexpressed idea that had so unnerved Emily
to-day.   To her consternation she discovered
that that comely figure was indelibly imprinted
in the centre of her nature still.

A host of bewildering questions, too, of a
more practical kind overwhelmed her. Granting
the occurrence an actual one, Emily could not
but persuade herself that Carr's eyes had looked
into her own with conscious recognition. What
was there involved in it? Was it the triumph
of four years' pursuit of her? . . . Was it the
result of ironical accident?   To Emily's reason-
ing the latter at any rate was impossible.   Carr
had never been a retail dispenser of small
personal mercies, therefore not likely to have
developed into a district visitor, even an un-
attached one.   Again how far and strangely

removed were these squalid fields of her own choosing from any of the probable haunts of the timber merchant of Millington. No, no, mere accident was impossible; what alternative therefore was alone irresistibly presented to her? ... Irresistible, probable, passing radiant as it was to her, Emily's soul sank before the acceptance of it. It was far, far too radiant for such as life had now become to her. Her reason dared not, would not submit to it, without at least some more precise and every-day a confirmation of it.

But the inflammable train of hope had become ignited, a train not easily to be quenched. The heroic effort of years was undermined, and Emily confronted her daily life with a single mind no longer.

We have had a glimpse of Carr's movements since the startling encounter, and know something of its effects upon him. Radically different as was the source of his emotion, his disquiet was little less than that of Emily. How it was affected or intensified by the course of events at Winwold we need not inquire. Utterly ignoble Theodore Carr was not; infected by a

pernicious epidemic of the moment he lived in
he may have been; but some constitution he
had beneath it all, and it might well be
that his ethic feebleness was due to the
ravages of fever rather than of organic disease.
Given this relic of sounder things, scoff at such
palpable puerilities as we may now do, fate is still
sometimes our imperious physician. But it is
not with alacrity that we submit to the physician's hand, or even admit the necessity of it.

From that day Emily found it scarcely possible to hide the change that had come over her.
Assured by her father that he could earn their
daily bread, since their establishment in Birmingham the girl had, with his consent and, in
so far as he was able, with his active co-opera-
tion, abandoned herself systematically to a path
in life rendered attractive, and under her altered
outlook necessary, to a devotional temperament.
With this disturbing spirit now again hovering
about her she was still unable to make any
outward change, but a great nervous strain was
put upon her. She could never leave her father's
door upon the simplest errand but in tremulous

fear of that alluring spectre. It seemed to rustle in the air and frustrate by its breath her most solid endeavour. She was condemned to turn corners fearfully, and start at the most unlikely encounters. Not highway or byway was secure to her, for go where she would she felt those eyes were constantly upon her.

But when a fortnight had passed, and she had not known any actual recurrence of the vision, the unrest became less acute. Beyond a certain point the most sensitive nature cannot go, if it have, that is, any conscious principle of life to be proof against the extravagances of hysteria. Emily had such principle in a very pronounced degree, and she became daily more conscious of its efficacy. It must not be supposed that it enabled her to regain what only through the fire of years she had acquired. For that doubtless an increased progression of years would be necessary, and then only providing that no recurrence of the disturbing factor should in the meantime assail her. But she at least got nearer to the compromise of life.

The immunity from disturbance, however, upon which all her strength depended was not allowed her. The third week had scarce elapsed ere another dart out of the obscurity reached her, and all previous effort was undone.

There was nothing extraordinary in Emily's receiving a letter. Her social activity had made her the recipient of sometimes two or three of a morning, from clergymen, philanthropic ladies, or even needy applicants to whom her propensities were now familiar. If her father chanced to take them in, he put them unexamined at a particular part of the mantelpiece to which the daughter's eyes first went upon her entering. So it was this day. It was afternoon, and Emily coming home found two such for her. She was in the room alone, and after examining their exterior she sat down before taking the next step. The handwriting upon one of them was familiar,—of a ghostly ante-natal familiarity touching unfathomable sensations. Poor Emily was tired, and before she could thrust her finger into the envelope she burst into a flood of tears over it.

When she had been able to regain some measure of calm, outward composure at any rate, she opened the letter. She drew out the contents, unfolded them, stared at them with a strange, confused expression of face, and let the rustling paper fall into her lap. It seemed with scant consciousness she fumbled in the empty envelope as though she had missed something, but without effect. Her hands again fell listlessly into her lap, and her vacant eyes rested upon what had come to her under the mocking guise of a letter. Two five-pound Bank of England notes! No other word accompanied them.

A few moments of this vacancy or reflection, whichever it was, sufficed, and Emily placed the money again in its envelope. She then got up, and began to prepare tea for her father. By the time they sat down she had succeeded n removing all traces of her recent emotion from her face.

When on the following day Emily was able to form a calmer estimate of this occurrence, she could not draw much comfort from it. She

would never have doubted from whom the
money came, even if she had not recognized
the handwriting, and this was where the sting
lay. It was not through the medium of coin
that she had ever looked for a renewal of intercourse with Theodore. If the fact did reveal
to her that his eyes had without her knowledge
followed her to her home, it also irresistibly proclaimed how he was altered . . . Could he
think that cash was the first thing she wanted
of him? That it was only in *that* that she had
lost by the deprivation of his companionship?
Perhaps Emily too had some far-away hidden
pride in her. The evil of the incident lay in
this; the good, in that it had imparted a daylight reality to that dreamlike vision which had
recently harassed her. It is always easier to
confront a fact than a fancy.

The money had been stowed away in a secret
receptacle without anything being said to Saloway about it, and Emily had lived through
another week. On the same day—it was Saturday—Emily found again the same handwriting
awaiting her. She opened the envelope more

resolutely upon this second occasion, and placed the one five-pound note that it contained with the others. The repetition of the experience was to prove that Emily's pride—if pride had been the emotion—was not impregnable. She was awake through the whole of the night succeeding, and in the review which the dark hours prompted she modified her position. We know that Emily's nature irresistibly leaned to charity. Had she not wronged Theodore? Might not his delicacy rather than the reverse have actuated his behaviour? A sudden meeting would, he knew, be disconcerting; he had detected her in her benevolent duties, had by indefatigable effort traced her to her home and calling,—was it not rather natural that he should seek a restoration of their intercourse by this surreptitious ministering to her unselfish instincts? Had he not constituted her his almoner rather than his pensioner,—intended these munificent sums for her joy in dispensing gladness to those in misery rather than for any common necessities of her own? This was far more like him.

This desired conclusion stood the test of day, and Emily immediately set about dispensing Carr's riches in consequence. Fifteen, twenty, twenty-five, thirty pounds she thus without difficulty disposed of, and another month had elapsed. Then her old scruples revived. Still no word from him; no further glimpse permitted. The cash began to be again put by.

After six months' regular reception of this five pounds weekly, every note of which had been silently added to the hoard in a box in Emily's bed-room, something further happened. This week the remittance arrived by the morning-post as it sometimes did, and Emily took it upstairs unopened when she went about her household work. In the vague reverie which alone it was now able to arouse in her, she chanced to stand by the window of her room with the envelope in her hand before opening it. She did not know that her eyes were looking out upon the street, that they were, as a matter of fact, resting upon the houses opposite. It was a wet, cloudy morning, and the pavements shone. There were a couple of hucksters' carts outside, the discordant voices of the owners audible. After the early departure of the artisan population to their daily labours, there were few other signs of life here through the day, except at meal times. The sound of a street-door, shut loudly, half consciously drew her attention, and where she looked her eyes remained. On the opposite pavement a man was raising his umbrella, and in the action he seemed to look directly into Emily's face. As though detected in some crime she shrank back, but the next minute pressed her face against the window-pane to watch to the farthest that departing figure. Unless her reason once again deceived her, she had beheld, for certain feverish seconds, the spectre, Theodore Carr . . . And he must be living there! And why?

In an instant all Emily's preconceptions of him were put to flight, and a wave of sympathetic affection overwhelmed her. Of every crime of faithlessness and ingratitude did she at once become convicted. By a flash of intuition all the heartless worldliness was hers; he the centre of all noblest tenderness. Emily's world was altered, and, in the course of the week, her father had to comment on it.

The money came as usual the following Saturday, and, very soon after its arrival, Emily went out. She passed down her own side of the street for some distance, then crossed and retraced her steps along the other pavement. At the door of No. 80 she stopped, and, whatever the condition of her nerves, she plied the knocker. Soon a woman came to answer it.

'Is Mr. Carr at home?'

'Who's Mr. Carr?'

'Doesn't he live here?'

'Nobody o' that name lives here. Try next door.'

The door was slammed without ceremony. Emily did try the next door, but her reception was more curt than at No. 80. So she went away in a haze of mystery.

Watch as she would, Emily could not again recapture that vision which had so disturbed her. The money came as usual, and was put away with the other, whilst Emily grew in the firm conviction that long brooding had made her the subject of delusions. With intenser energy she sought the refuge of devotion and works of charity. If at any time what seemed a shadow flitted away from the pavement as she came home in the darkness, she hardly noticed it. Spectres of all kinds began to lose their power over her.

For two years things thus continued, the money regularly arriving, but not a syllable of explanation to accompany it. The notes had become mere paper to Emily, and the putting them away a pure matter of form. But that the envelopes were still addressed in that known handwriting, she could just as easily have put the money into the fire. Young though she was, Emily had never been robust, and the course of her life began at this time to tell considerably upon her health. She had long practised every kind of self-denial, whether in mere resistance of bodily fatigue or in the giving away her own dinner. It became obvious to her father that she was frequently suffering, or, at any rate, far from well. Since her attainment to womanhood she had painfully struck Saloway by a strong physical resemblance to her mother during her days of trial, and this depressed the cobbler unspeakably. Depression in Benjamin invariably sapped his energies, and perhaps it was partly owing to this that his petty commercial affairs (never of a wide margin of prosperity) went badly with him. The savings from his prosperous days in Millington had for some time been exhausted, and, try to hoodwink himself as he might, it was becoming but too apparent that there was an increasing difficulty in meeting the bare weekly needs. *It was just at the dawning of this fact definitely upon Saloway that Emily fell ill.

She was confined to her bed for a week, and the exceptional outlay to which the cobbler was put could leave him in no sort of doubt as to the financial problem. It chanced that on the Saturday afternoon, as Saloway was considering what other article he could conveniently dispose of in order to procure the necessary delicacy for his daughter's Sunday food, the postman came. The cobbler took the letter in,—

there was only one,—and contrary to his custom he examined the envelope. It was more the heedless play of nervousness than any fixed intention, but in whatever spirit undertaken it was soon serious enough. Benjamin stared at the paper, and trembled from head to foot. Emily, too, in her bedroom had heard the postman, and she called from upstairs.

'Only one, Emily,' said Saloway, as he shuffled into the room.

She took it from his hand, saw it to be the expected one, and laid it on the counterpane. Then her eyes rose calmly to her father's. Seeing his expression, she read it rightly, and her thin face was suffused with a deep colour.

'See what he says, father,' said she, pointing to the envelope; and Benjamin silently obeyed.

With tremulous fingers he tore it open, took out the five-pound note, which he let fall from his hand, and searched for the more precious document behind. Finding the envelope empty, as Emily too upon her first occasion had done, he looked into his daughter's face, and muttered,

'Ne'er a word, maidie.'

Surprise could no longer assail Emily, so she only smiled; but the next moment a tear rolled down her cheek, once again pale, and there was a minute's silence.

'What be the meaning of it?' asked Saloway, as though waking from a dazed condition.

'That he never wishes to see us again,' replied Emily, with a calm, but firmly uttered conviction, never formulated until that moment.

The quiet decisiveness took Benjamin aback, for to him this was the first ray of communication across a dark void of expectant years, and so instantaneous a construction of it was not in keeping with his own habits of mind. But he had come to have an almost childlike dependence upon the mental superiority of his daughter, and he accepted her opinions without question.

'Then we can't use this money, Emily, I count,' was all his comment.

'No, we can't, father. Give it to me.'

There is strange spiritual intercommunion between those that live very much and very exclusively together, leading to intuitive readings of the mind from what were but a vacant page to a stranger. Emily felt a flash of this as the paper passed to her own hand from that of her father, and she looked up at him.

'You are not in want of it, father?' she asked, quickly.

'No, no, maidie, never fear.'

When dusk fell, Saloway went out shopping. Emily lay reflecting in her bed.

By the middle of the following week Emily could crawl about again, but her strength returned to her slowly. She read much in books of devotion, but would sometimes sit for an hour at a time in listless idleness. It was not Carr now that occupied her attention, but her father. She was unable to rid her mind of that ugly impression which had so unaccountably possessed her. Having once occurred, there was so much ready to rush in upon her and confirm the worst. She wondered that certain things could so long have escaped her. When she began to dust the rooms again, she missed sundry articles long familiar to her, but dared not put any inquiry. Long immersed

in her own absorbing topics, she had scarcely
given a practical thought to the common
problem of her own existence. The small sums
necessary for so humble an establishment had
always been forthcoming, with even modest
contributions to her charitable fund upon occasion. That this should be altering was naturally not easy of immediate comprehension.

But upon the brink of so startling an emerg-
ency Emily did not linger long. She was resolved to spare her father the anguish of another
explanation, so she formed her own conclusions
and laid her own plans in complete independence
of him. One morning, when her strength permitted it, she went out.

Emily's efforts proved successful, and with the
aid of a philanthropic lady with whom her
charitable work had brought her in contact, she
at once obtained employment. This was at a
wholesale stationery establishment where Emily
became merged in the ranks of those who
gummed and folded envelopes. But the consciousness of the needful increment would have
sustained her through very much worse than

this. Indeed, her health showed definite improvement under it, and life soon accommodated itself to the new channel. Thenceforth only on Sundays and after working hours did Emily find time for her works of mercy, but No. 159 was rescued, and therein Emily could discern mercy enough.

CHAPTER XV.

IN THE BALANCE.

I.

ONE windy September night, with gusts of rain dashing against his face, Clarke trudged wearily along the pavement of Primrose Hill towards his lodgings at No. 80. Upwards of two years now had he retained this room, and he had frequently to confess to himself that it had not supplied him with all that he had wished from it. The man had been conscious latterly of increased repugnance for the locality and all that it implied in life ; a feeling which, as now, rose sometimes to a height of intolerable loathing.

Let the rain beat as it might, he was unable

to turn into his shelter. He strode along the interminable pavement, fleeing from he scarcely knew what, seeking that which he could define no better. The negative possessed his veins, veins which were adapted only to a very definite affirmative. There was nothing exceptional in his disorganized condition; the exception merely lay in his inability to neutralize the mischief by a homœopathic dose of artificial sensation.

In a world of practical endeavour, whose eye tips a nose of faultless projection, momentary indecision is viewed with contempt; a two years' indecision doubtless with boisterous vilification. For upwards of two years had it been Clarke's daily intention to call at No. 159 opposite, and it was an intention still.

At length by the side of a lamp-post Clarke stopped, and looked consciously forward into the dim perspective stretching endless before him. To his present state of mind it suggested the grimmest of vistas, and he recoiled from it. Too possibly it reflected the chaos of his own soul, a prospect upon which he could never dwell with much delight. With the same kind of impulsive movement that had characterized his steps hitherto, the man suddenly crossed the street, and set off on his return journey down the other pavement.

Without the slightest hesitation he stopped in front of No. 159. There was no light in any of the windows, but he did not at first notice that. He stepped up to the door and knocked. As there was no response, he repeated the summons louder. This still remaining unanswered, he cast his eye over the front of the building and noticed it was dark. The window of the house adjoining was a-light, so he knocked at that door. Yes, Mr. Saloway did live at No. 159. There was nobody in, then. That was possible, for the father went out every evening, and since the daughter had gone to work she was never in before eight o'clock, sometimes later; but would he leave a message?

'The daughter goes out to work, does she?' he asked, in astonishment.

'Yes, sir,'—Clarke was in his best clothes, and looked pre-eminently respectable although wet,—'has done for two or three months.'

'Thank you, I needn't leave a message. I—I'll call again.'

The visitor went some distance down the street, then returned directly to No. 80.

When in the light of his own room the expression of Clarke's face denoted unmistakable anger. There was a promptitude apparent, too, in his movements with which these walls were not familiar, and which seemed to astonish the landlady when she appeared, anxious to know his wishes. Upon the table were gathered several of his personal possessions from the walls and mantel-piece, and into a box which had always been stowed away under a side table he was in the act of packing his books.

'Yes, I shall want some tea . . . And, Mrs. Ellis, I shall have to leave to-night. For good, I am afraid. Of course I shall pay you for a month's notice. I have to go to Manchester.'

'Lor, Mr. Clarke, I'm sorry to hear that.'

'Yes, I'm sorry, but it seems inevitable.'

After a few more words the woman went to make the tea, and Clarke resumed his packing.

His resolution did not again desert him. Through all the months that Clarke had contemplated that house opposite, not once until this moment had he regarded it with other than sympathy and solicitude. He had paced before it in the darkness, (fleeing from the vaguest shadow that approached its doorway,) and watched it by the hour from the security of his curtained window, weaving all sorts of tender fancies about the unsuspecting inmates, and investing them with all the idyllic halo of an ideal future: and the mere discovery that the daughter worked could in an instant change all that. It can hardly be supposed that Clarke resented work as derogatory to his ideal of humanity, but whatever his interpretation of it the result was as stated. He was angry. His disgust with the locality, with the purpose for which he sought it, and with the whole phase of life that it implied, was complete. He could resist it no longer, and flight was an imperative need. When the tea was laid, he had done his packing. His meal was a pretence. He thrust some of the bread into his pocket to make believe that he had eaten it, daubed the uncleaned knife with butter in obvious disgust, and mixed some tea in his cup. For the few minutes that he would have been engaged he stared about the vulgar appointments of the room and muttered audibly.

A quarter of an hour later the wheels of a cab were heard rattling over the stones of Primrose Hill, an unusual sound for that locality, and then all was left to the wind and rain again.

II.

For some time Carr's world had deemed his behaviour uncommonly erratic. In view of his extraordinary good fortune at so early an age, this did not in itself exactly excite surprise; what chiefly occasioned comment was the air of mystery that seemed to hang over his youthful errantries. The courses of the ordinary mortal under such enviable circumstances can be foreseen with some measure of exactness, as they generally lie over one or other of the very well-beaten tracks. In Carr's case this was not seen to be so, irregularity in his attendance at business being the only apparent point at which he touched the common route. When he fled abroad, it was rumoured that he had started a yacht; this collapsing, he was made the purchaser of the parish of Winwold, and the intention of inaugurating a new race of squires there was at once attributed to him. This in its turn had to give way to the haze of indeterminate speculation.

The fact was that, directly, nothing was popularly known of Carr and his propensities, for he played no social part, and could number his friends on the fingers of one hand. That he was a fine-art connoisseur was of course generally accepted, but none of his colossal purchases were publicly chronicled, so that there was no ground for supposing that he was developing this.

Carr himself was in the meantime no less mystified than the most envious of his neighbours. Bluntly confronted with the question, he could not have told you what he was doing. From a life of definite purpose and high endeavour he had at a plunge become immersed in a welter of indecision and uncertainty. At particularly lucid moments he would ponder the fact, and shudder at it. There was something on his mind that he wanted to do, of that he was intolerably conscious, but not for the life of him could he carry it into action. Yawning gulfs opened before him when he raised his foot upon what seemed solid road to him, and for immolation in gulfs Theodore had never known any faculty. Thus it was that the raised foot came to be continually drawn back again.

Two friends, indeed, Carr had by this time acquired, but neither seemed to be of any assistance to him at this juncture. These were Lindred, the artist, and Galbraith, the literary man; two natures of very different calibre, but each making definite appeal to something in Theodore's nature. To Winwold he occasionally still went for a Sunday: the conjunction with Galbraith in London had been made and continued. But the fact was that Theodore Carr was one of those afflicted mortals (significantly increasing in our day) condemned to the desert of essential solitude. They may number friends, but they expand not; the heart-strings being constricted by the chill oversight of intellectual scruples. Intercourse becomes a tragically superficial matter. With the exception of Laura Blakenhurst, Carr had not set eyes on the mortal to whom he could reveal his soul.

In this period of tribulation, Carr naturally leaned rather to the nomadic Galbraith than to the placid and stationary Lindred. The vagabondage and versatility of the contemporary imaginative nature (fairly typified in Galbraith) appealed strongly to momentary sensations of revolt which characterised this transitional period in Carr. Aware of nothing disgraceful in Galbraith, even according to the most antiquated standards, still was there an engaging emancipation in his habits of action and of thought which to Theodore's restricted experience of real life came with all the pleasure of discovery. By the countenance which it gave to recent impressions in himself, it added a new dignity to impulses which he had formerly regarded with more or less dismay.

Late one wet September night, Carr arrived in

Millington from one of his mysterious journeys, and as it was too late for a visit to his timber-yard he went directly to his rooms. Judging by his looks and actions he was not in the best of moods, and he regarded a pile of letters awaiting him with audible impatience. By a dash of the hand he spread them, like one might do a pack of cards, and from the lot his eye quickly selected one only. This he at once tore open.

'DEAR CARR,'—it ran,—'I came to Wolver-hampton on Friday by the ten a.m. from Pad-dington. May I hope for your company in an interesting exploration? Yours,

'OWEN GALBRAITH.'

It was now Thursday. Carr went to town by the sleeping car on the mail train a couple of hours later, and the next morning he met Gal-braith at Paddington. They travelled to Wolver-hampton in company, and, after a couple of exhilarating days there, Theodore took his friend with him to Millington.

They arrived in the evening, and dinner was ready for them. When Carr came from his room he gave a glance at the dinner-table, gave a few words of instruction to the maid, and then went himself to fetch up the wine. On re-entering the dining-room, he did not for an instant see Galbraith, then his eye became aware of the back of him. The poet had immediately detected some good paintings on the walls, and had been engaged with one of them before Carr's entrance.

'Now, sir—— You approve of that?'

'It is by no common artist,' said Galbraith, coming towards the table.

Carr laughed acquiescence, and before taking his seat, put light to a lamp which was evidently suspended and shaded with the sole object of throwing light upon the one picture they had referred to. It consequently afforded the first topic of conversation. Carr descanted volubly on the merits of the artist in question ; Galbraith on the purely artistic merits of the picture.

'My only objection would be,' added the latter at one point, 'that there is just a trace of vindictiveness in the artist, the result probably of lack of appreciation of the real character of the original.'

' You think so ?' laughed Carr.   'Not arising from disappointed affection ?'

'I should say not, but it might be either.'

'I believe you were right at first; the latter it can hardly be in view of Lindred's age and placid philosophy.   I think, as you say, the real character is not exactly to his standard, and so he has unduly emphasized certain traits.   As a matter of fact, the lady is now married and gone abroad.   He is disappointed in her.'

'They of the old dispensation might be; that woman is for the future.'

Carr ruminated this remark in silence, his commonplace word or two not really breaking it. A few minutes later he interposed the remark,

'Then there is antagonism between the old and the future ?'

'The everlasting one between light and darkness.'

Carr did not contest the assertion, but it gave him food for reflection at such moments as he was alone.   The thought had vaguely occurred to him before in the course of his development, and with particular reference to the relative temperaments of Theodore Carr and Laura Blakenhurst; but he had not put it so dogmatically. Lindred he knew was of another opinion. As the wine circulated, Carr favoured Galbraith and Laura. The acceptance of the poet's dogma undoubtedly stimulated his host's conversation, a certain recklessness being apparently necessary for Carr's fullest intellectual play. A brilliant evening was passed over cigars and Theodore's artistic collections.

Galbraith had two days at his friend's service, and a visit to Winwold was agreed upon. Before leaving in the morning, Carr went to his office, as he did at sufficiently frequent intervals, to enable him to keep in touch with the reins of commercial activity there, and it chanced that he found one of his partners in the act of setting off to find him, or at least discover if he were at home. By way of explanation, a business letter was put into his hand, which, to Carr's astonishment, was dated from the 'Five Gables, Winwold.' It was brief, and merely requested a private interview with Mr. Carr upon an important commercial transaction, being subscribed by 'Yours faithfully, George H. Hascard.'

'Yes, I know him by repute,—a speculative solicitor. He has recently gone to live there; but why should he write on business from his private residence, and on Sunday?'

However, Carr was going to Winwold, and undertook to attend to the matter. He was of course accustomed now to commercial solicitations in his capacity of prominent capitalist.

Once away, Carr did not make so light of the occurrence as he had affected to do. Anything connected with Winwold disquieted him still, and he had not mentioned a fact with which he was familiar, namely, that this same Hascard was the family solicitor of Squire Blakenhurst. This might be of slight or no significance, but to Theodore's present mood it was considerable.

This he dismissed for the moment, and in a state of apparent exhilaration he sped with his companion across the autumn country, glorying in the golds and greys that the placid landscape so lavishly presented. The three or four miles from Gosstall station, spanning the upland

pastures which rose around the village of Winwold, they had arranged to walk. At noon
they alighted on the quiet platform, the little
station embodying itself for them in the rank
of black frost-bitten dahlias and tall sun-flowers
with faces down which skirted the long white
palisade. It was a clear, sunny, shadowy day,
with scarce a breath of wind; snow-white
crested clouds sailing majestically over bluest
space. Both of the travellers felt the influence
of the scene, and they took the road blithely.

Around them lay a picturesquely wooded
landscape, of some diversity of outline, backed
by stretches of bare open wold in the direction
in which they walked, whereon a grey stone
barn, a fir-tree or a beech, stood out clearly
amongst the geometrical lines of wall. Their
own road passed between that fir clump on the
farthest ridge, in which at this distance the
passage appeared as a little cut against the
blue sky. Carr at least felt younger here. The
placidity of the sunlit country road fell as a
balm upon his soul. The artificial stress of life
was not obtruded upon his sight. All sorts of

other healthier ideals could be for the moment harboured and sustained, finding sanction in all the silent fragrant influences which every leaf and blade exhaled. As a consequence he spoke but little. A magpie that flew chattering away could instantly dispel a topic.

Very little of directly human suggestion did they encounter on the way. For some distance it was a green-margined road with hedges of blackberries and rose hips on either side, and ash and beech leaves scattered over the surface. Under a horse-chestnut tree Galbraith would stop to pick up the cracked prickly husks and extract the mahogany white-tonsured nuts from their cosy beds. In a quarry opening from the roadside, the exhausted half of which was a sombre grove of tall silent larch-trees, an ancient and solitary labourer was at work; another was breaking stones by a wall skirting a turnip-field; a robin sang from a bush of clematis; a wheeling kestrel uttered its deceptive plaint; and then from that ridge towards which from the first they had been aiming, the village of Winwold lay just before them, on the wooded slope leading to still further ridges beyond.

Here Carr halted to display his prospect: a prospect which still he could never behold without a peculiar thrill of deep proprietary emotion. Galbraith was astonished. The richness of the land surprised him, the bare stony uplands ending almost abruptly where he stood. There were luxuriant pastures before him; fine trees in the brilliance of every variety of autumn hue, and stubble on which stood shocks of grain still to be carried. After interchange of appropriate enthusiasm, they went on. Having descended the slope, they entered the irregular street of grey stone gabled and mullioned cottages, many overgrown with various creepers, and each with its garden of hollyhocks, chrysanthemums, and sunflowers, and came to the 'Frog Mill Inn,' which fronted the spacious village green, in the centre of which was a shattered elm-tree, the gnarled, cleft, decapitated old trunk alone possessing one great arm stretched out pathetically towards the heavens.

After partaking of such homely fare as the inn could afford, and for which their walk had made them ready, Carr took his friend off to see Mr. Lindred. On arriving at Farbarrow, however, they found to their disappointment that the artist was in Orkney, so they had to spend the afternoon in another walk on their own account. They took the 'Five Gables' in their course, and Carr learned that Mr. Hascard would be at home to dinner at seven, whereat it would give him pleasure to have the company of Mr. Carr: an invitation which was as graciously accepted.

When in the evening accordingly Galbraith was left alone, he sought the diversion of the vernacular conversation which he heard proceeding in the common room of the inn, where some half-a-dozen countrymen were assembled. Immediately before his entry, it chanced that he himself, as the unknown companion of Mr. Carr, had been the subject of discussion.

'A artist, Gearge,' had been the verdict of one of the observers in the company.

'To be sure, I could see that in his hair, Thomas, in a minute. But a civil-spoken man a be, quite.'

'Quite so. It be uncommon strange what——'

As the door opened and Galbraith walked in, all faces were turned upon him in silence, and there was a murmured response to his ready greeting. He took one of the wooden chairs and drew it up to the settle.

'Plenty of room, don't move,' said he. 'Got a match?' so he put a light to his pipe.

Galbraith entered with gusto into the spirit of the place, talking affably upon every sort of local topic. The story of the squire and his family he had soon elicited, and, when he heard it, he fancied that his friend Carr had displayed some reticence in his casual references to it. Blending with the idyllic atmosphere which, throughout the day, had so pleasantly impressed him, the poet owned a singular fascination in this mouldering Winwold, and its imaginative capabilities began actively to assert themselves. For the hours ensuing he gave himself up unreservedly to their influence.

The clock had struck ten when Carr returned, and, as his companions had departed, Galbraith was found reclining in the settle, in amicable conversation with the landlady's daughter. Carr joined them with a thoughtful countenance, which his best efforts were not able altogether to lighten.

The enterprising Hascard had, for some time, sought a favourable opportunity of bringing himself to young Carr's notice. The opportunity had come, not quite in the manner that he had expected, but, since he was not a man of any inconvenient degree of sensibility, it would serve as well as (perhaps, he thought, better than) another. He received Carr with well-bred cordiality, but not until they were alone with cigars in his study did the lawyer broach the particular subject of the hour.

'You haven't made the personal acquaintance of our squire, Mr. Carr?'

Carr had not; had not understood that there was likely to be any compatibility between their respective worlds.

'No, no, I think not. He is quite an old stager. But one must feel sympathy for the old man. That remarkable escapade of his daughter has quite unhinged him. He would have sacrificed all the rest of his family to retain her.'

'H'm . . .'

'I sometimes think that he has closed his account with life through it . . . His recklessness amounts to lunacy.'

'Financial recklessness?'

'That is all which my profession takes cognizance of,' smiled the lawyer. 'It is gross injustice to Vivian, the heir, but my best efforts are unavailing. I once suggested a full discussion with Mr. Vivian about the state of affairs —I thought I had committed apoplectic murder. It is no breach of confidence to tell you that he threatened to transfer the whole of his affairs to another adviser if Vivian got so much as wind of his affairs. What can one do? In other hands matters would be hopeless. The fact is, he is now intent upon disposing of the timber. If I decline to do the negotiations, he will himself do it surreptitiously, and heaven only knows into what hands he will fall.'

'What, he wants to dispose of the timber to

be felled,' exclaimed Carr, rising in his chair, 'all the timber—here ?'

'Such is his serious proposal.'

'But why doesn't he sell the estate rather? What is it worth without the trees ?'

Hascard shrugged his shoulders, and eyed Carr through the smoke which he had driven from his lips. Carr himself was, as by some magic process, transported to the green recesses amidst the lower boughs of one of the trees referred to, and, for an extensive dealer in the commodity, certainly admitted a very sentimental vein of reflection. It was the lawyer's business to divine his guest's attitude, and turn it to his own account accordingly. This Mr. Hascard was able to do with greater ease than he had thought probable. The fact was that Carr's sensation was too genuine to admit of disguise, even if he had been minded to attempt it. The proposal came to him with all the vehemence of a personal calamity.

'But can't the man be brought to see the gross absurdity——'

'That would be its greatest recommendation.'

'Then, if he is mad, can't the law restrain him from acting?'

'We couldn't prove absolute dementia,' laughed Hascard.

'Evidence does not seem wanting . . . But of course I should be prepared to treat.'

'Ha, you would? Armed with that assurance I shall feel satisfied, so far as one can in such a deplorable case. If you can surreptitiously form an estimate of the value of the timber it would be kind. Should the squire come across checkered poles and note-books upon his estate, the consequence would, I am convinced, be tragical. He himself will communicate with you direct: it may be in a mouth, it may be in twelve. Such is his condition.'

The few moments' reflection had presented things in a still stronger light to Carr, and he began to fear that he had not made his own ground strong enough.

' I will undertake to do it secretly,' he said, with more animation. 'I will do it myself, in fact. It shall not be done through my office; so will you address in future to my private residence? You understand I should not like the transaction to escape me, so you may calculate upon rather more than strictly commercial dealings. I would go to the utmost possible value, so long as I indemnify myself from——'

'To be sure, to be sure,—no actual loss. You are generous, Mr. Carr. You will pardon my saying that report had prepared me for delicacy of this kind from you. I don't care for business after dinner, so let this suffice. You can spare us the night? I have an engagement in Millington in the morning, and we might——'

Carr interposed his engagement at the 'Frog Mill.'

'Then an hour or two. Shall we go into the drawing-room? I always like to end the day——'

And the gentlemen exchanged the dense atmosphere of commerce and tobacco fumes for the fragrant presence of Mrs. Hascard and her daughter Gwendoline.

The next morning, contrary to his wont, Carr slept late, and, what was equally unaccustomed,

Galbraith was up half-an-hour before sunrise. The poet had projected a magazine paper upon the awakening of the sun which the idyllic circumstances had prompted in him, and accordingly, at the moment registered by the calendar for that suggestive phenomenon, Galbraith was stationed at the White Lady's Clump, a picturesque group of beech-trees crowning the ridge, to take his observations. When Carr came down to breakfast he heard with some surprise of his friend's expedition, and of the fact that the gentleman wished Mr. Carr to begin, as he was writing in his bed-room and might be some little time. Just as Carr was finishing what had at best been an apology for a breakfast, Galbraith came in hilariously to join him, with a letter for post in his hand.

The words, the ink whereof was as yet scarcely dry, were these :

'The " Frog Mill Inn,"<br>'Winwold, Gloucestershire.

'DEAR ——,

   'Is the enclosed of any use to you? It is not bunkum, and has been literally this moment written at the seat of sunrise and under its direct inspiration.

'The man Carr of whom I spoke to you has done me a considerable service by bringing me to this place, the very name of which aptly reveals to you some of its brave qualities. It is exactly the spot I have wanted for occasional rustication, and to show you that I am in earnest I may tell you that I have just secured a cottage here on a seven years' lease. Grey lichened stone, with two gables to the front, which from foundation to roof is overgrown with ivy, honeysuckle, clematis, roses, and another thing which is just now a blaze of scarlet berries. A flower garden, kitchen garden, and some half acre of green orchard. For this, fifteen pounds per annum! But you shall see it.

'If you want any rustic articles now and then you know where to turn. I shall be up day after to-morrow, so address to 49.

'Yours,

'O. G.'

Carr received his friend's enthusiastic announcement without any corresponding fervour. Indeed, had Theodore been able to reveal his mind, a very complex state of emotion would have been discovered there. He was somewhat preoccupied, it is true, but that did not prevent a very positive turn of feeling in him. In plain terms he resented this action of Galbraith.

Despite the abdication of the divinity, Winwold was still more of a creed to Theodore than he would have been willing to admit. All his relationship with the locality was of an extremely serious and emotional kind, too deep for any disturbance from surface ruffling, and to see another lighter temperament able to step in and enjoy the cream, so to speak, from very idleness, irritated Carr. The jealousy of extreme susceptibility was no doubt at the root of the sensation; intolerance of any more frivolous conception of existence than he was himself possessed of. Without his in the least suspecting it, Carr's temperament was profoundly and insurmountably religious, however indeterminate the dogmas whereon it was founded. In Galbraith, as in the general intelligence of his moment, the religious faculty was adulterated to non-existence. Perhaps only by this particular juncture could Theodore have learned where such subtle antipathies joined issue.

The discovery, however, was of course only for his own benefit, and a short time enabled him to accommodate himself to his friend's requirements. The morning was spent in what remained to complete the poet's bargain, and Carr was able to sustain it without any flagrant betrayal of his condition. When they wandered over the country, he talked much of the trees with a highly poetical rather than a commercial suggestion, and when not speaking of them his eyes seemed to dwell upon very little else in the landscape. Just as his coming, so was Galbraith's departure, an infinite relief to Theodore, and when again alone he spent two reflective days in the silent byways of Winwold.

He seemed in those two days to regain several of the threads which his recent life had entirely lost. His soul returned to the devotional aspect

of the mere universe; to the inspiring natural
attributes of mother earth. Once again he
sought out the Swinging Tree, that great um-
brageous wych-elm from whose recesses he had
looked out upon the generous enthusiasm of
Laura, the logical prosecution of which he himself could never doubt to be the only rational
explanation of her later errantries. The leaves
which had so kindly screened him were now
thin and mellow, but he climbed up to his old
shelter, and by force of association, (always
peculiarly powerful in him,) recalled the hap-
pier dispensation of those former days. The
buoyant Carr was conscious of supremest failure
in all that he had held the crown of life whilst
being at the same time conscious that his life
had hardly yet begun. Until he had seen
Laura he had barely known the meaning of
solitude, (save for that momentary but indelible
impression at his mother's death); having seen
her he had found the ideal antidote to the sting
which she had herself occasioned; having lost
her, the poison had found a free current through

his veins, to the stemming of which all his feverish vagaries had contributed little more than the hollowest of mockeries. The wealth, whereto as means he had attached so exclusive an importance, was his in undreamed-of abundance, and its golden teeth rattled ironically in the jaws which had expanded into that broad and ghastly grin. He found that he was solitary still.

Trees, like waves, have a remarkable faculty of attuning their notes to the heart-strings of the hearer: scarcely the platitude which insensibility may adjudge it, since the lesser chords of Nature are constant, for dule or for joy. Carr had learned this before, in effect if not by conscious examination. Thus now did the leaves give forth to him tones of muffled solemnity, although it was a sparkling north-west that played them. What might have been a glee was a silvery dirge, which owned through its melancholy cadence an irresistible power of soothing. Despite his material occupation with them, Carr had throughout his life been peculiarly sensitive to the spiritual influence of trees.

This feeling he now found to have been indefinitely deepened. Under the sense of solitude to which his soul had become subjected he knew a fresh and unsuspected source of consolation in an abandonment to these purely natural sources. Not to the merely æsthetic interpretation of them, still less to the merely human association through which he had for so many years exclusively beheld them. It was to the elemental germ that he had penetrated, to the point where his own inscrutable being blended with the mysterious winds of heaven, whereof you may hear the sound but know not whence they come nor whither they may lead you.

This transcendental experience had more than a fleeting effect upon Carr. It is true that it was not consistently maintained in his immediate daily practice, else would he never have retraced his steps to the dusty highway of the world; but it materially affected his habits of mind in the privacy of his own reflections. It had registered a spiritual point from which there was no human possibility of receding.

It to some extent calmed the restless current of his existence, if it established no very positive safeguard for its future course. Through it he came to regard the prospective transaction with regard to the Winwold trees with an imaginative mysticism savouring strongly of religious obligation. The threatened destruction of them caused him as much agitation as an act of gravest sacrilege, and he was impatient to interpose his own reverent authority between the venerated object and the hand of the insensible destroyer. In this the squire did not seem inclined to humour him, for as the weeks extended to months, and as month after month went by, the looked-for communication never came.

In the course of the following year, in response to one more inquiry, Mr. Hascard had to announce a further indefinite postponement of the affair, as his unfortunate client, Mr. Blakenhurst, had sustained a severe paralytic seizure upon the field of St. Leger, and there was great uncertainty as to what the issue might be.

'In either contingency, however,' added the lawyer, significantly, '*something* will have to be done in the course of the next few months.'

So it eventually proved.

CHAPTER XVI.

BY THE SS. 'KARROO.'

As the vessel passed the Needles, exchanging the rolling swell of the Channel for the calm of narrower shores, a lady stepped out from the companion doorway to the deck, and for an instant, dazed by the scene which met her, abruptly stopped. Recovering herself, she advanced to the side, and raised one hand to the level of her rippling eyebrows.

All the water was aglow with the crimson radiance of a sinking October sun, and beyond lay the English coast-line in a halo of mystic and profound light. A thrill of emotion passed through this woman's heart as she continued to gaze westwards, but, as she was aware of the glance of other passengers turned from the scene upon herself, there was no danger of any outward betrayal of her feelings. Major Kennet, one of these passengers, a middle-aged gentleman of unimpeachable appearance, had taken a few hurried steps forward as the lady came forth, but he too stopped short. Immediately, the waggish Miss Felling nudged her mother to look at the major struggling to impart to his own pose and features a proper degree of poetic expression, and her mother could not repress a smile, suggestively carrying her eyes on to that other lady also as she did so. The gallant major had, throughout the voyage, been jocularly regarded as the self-constituted cavalier of this Mrs. Chatwin, who travelled alone and, despite the appearance of wealth and dignity which her person and appointments alike presented, wholly unattended. But he had felt instinctively repelled by the aspect of solemn reflection with which now, silent and apart, she regarded the sunset, and he was obliged to withhold for the moment the characteristic pleasantries with which such natural phenomena had been heretofore received.

Whatever the instances of individual sentiment, the excitement incidental to a long-expected landing soon surged uppermost, and, amongst the general company, the busy movements and brisk, short utterances of preparation for the shore effectually dispelled the imaginative attitude. Nurses and governesses ran about the deck, up steps, down steps, peering into every possible forbidden corner, impatiently summoning their charges to the detested toilet. There was much jostling with good-humoured nods and apologies on the companion-way; gentlemen folding rugs complacently, to the general inconvenience, in the narrowest spaces; ladies with flushed and eager faces enjoining Tom and Ned on no account to forget——; younger, more self-conscious ladies smiling critically at the general confusion to emphasize their own wiser calm and unconcern.

But the major perceived that the passenger of his especial interest held aloof from all this popular commotion, and detected in her, as he thought, a very notable change.   Hitherto she had, at any rate, graciously acquiesced in his polite attentions, even approving his facetious exuberance by an intellectual pleasantry which ravished the soldier.   Mrs. Chatwin, he always after averred, was in no way the same after that first glimpse of the English sunset coast.   Venturing at length to approach her, to all his remarks and kindly officiousness she presented a constrained, not to say repressive demeanour. Might he not get her——?   Oh, no, her personal incumbrances were nothing.   There was a singular appearance of reserve in such general remarks as the major was able to extort.   The lady was preoccupied, and gazed obliviously towards the land.

'And through the customs—you will allow me—ha, but of course somebody will meet you here?'

She smiled, but made no direct response. Was not the major overstepping the bounds of civilised behaviour?   They were no longer in the chartered liberty of the high seas.   The man positively repeated his hint as to the unconventional situation. She showed displeasure at his pertinacity.

'I shall not be met at Southampton, Major Kennet,' she said, brusquely, turning further away.

The gentleman lifted his eyebrows in genuine dismay and, no doubt, unaffected solicitude.

'Then, at the risk of your highest displeasure,' cried he, 'I must see you through their hands. This place, Mrs. Chatwin,—they boast of it, but believe me, the insolence of the *canaille* is un-paralleled. Talk of Italians—nay, of Boers and Zulus——'

The major expanded his palms expressively, a travelled gesture habitual with him.

'Do you hear, Miss Felling?' said the major's victim, adroitly appealing to the young lady, who was passing. 'Here is Major Kennet re-viling your English officials. Surely you will never allow it?'

'Oh, major, that is too unkind,' returned Miss Felling, with unconcealed sarcasm ;—she was a blonde young lady who blushed, and who, so said the deck gossips, had been anxious to share

the good will of the soldier with Mrs. Chatwin,
or, as some hinted, even to divert it into a more
exclusive channel. The gentleman, in politeness, had never disguised his aversion for Miss
Felling. There was a shade of tragic discomfiture, therefore, in his eyes as they followed the
elder lady who, under cover of this manœuvre,
took to flight, and disappeared amidst the
throng by the companion doorway. Miss Felling saw it, and smiled openly as Major Kennet
abruptly discovered how important it was to
gather together his own possessions also, and
therewith to leave her with scarcely dignified
abruptness.

When Mrs. Chatwin ventured again to emerge,
the scene had altered. The great vessel was in
still calmer water, and seemed to smile with
giant pride as she ploughed her way through
the glittering ripples into the roads, contemptuously conscious of her strength, but only by
the way of ostentatious dalliance finding occasion to exert it. Other great craft and small
were there to see her, to eye her with interest,
for she was from the Cape and two days late. The

sea-gulls with short scream and croak kept swooping around her; and the coast-line with its fringe of yellow sand, so strangely placid and stationary, was diversified with the various familiar suggestions of human enterprise. The lady gazed at it with undiminished ardour, and allowed her intellectual sensibility to play in ripples about her eyelids and over her smooth wide forehead. The last rim of the sun had disappeared, and now in the evening light the sky was clearing. In the west lay numberless streaks of thin clouds, rosy pink, whilst a single narrow belt of the same hue girded the blue heavens in the south, with the clear half moon above it, and the landscape in a mist of damson bloom below—the homely English landscape.

This time she was permitted to indulge her reverie uninterrupted, for the major had resolved no longer directly to obtrude his services, and everybody else was far too busy to be concerned on her account. The gallant gentleman busied himself over his own baggage with ostentatious exclusiveness, even to the last moment of the

groaning, backing, and sidling necessary to the
bringing of the unwieldy vessel to her proper
moorings. When she was fairly alongside, and
the steady panting of the engines announced
the completion of their long heroic task, Major
Kennet hurried forth and cast his eagle glance
upon the crowded gangways and the busy
throng beyond. Artificial lights were beginning
to obscure the autumn twilight, and wholly to
extinguish the subtle tints of sky and water
which had engaged the attention of one or two
of the passengers until now. The scene here
presented was distinctly human, in supremest
contrast to that which these travellers by the
Karroo had beheld for so many days. To the
major the contrast was wholly gratifying. He
took in at a glance the active commonplace
crowd on the quay, and the blank masonry beyond. He sought no face in the expectant
throng, and primarily a man of the world, and
an extensively travelled one, naturally he knew
none of the imaginative emotions which might
be stirring more susceptible bosoms upon step-

ping towards the land. One emotion alone was agitating him. He was angrily intent upon counteracting the evil machinations of those he would only recognize as 'Southampton dock ruffians,' so far as they should be put in practice against the unsuspecting object of his care. As he had expected, the lady herself held back until the main company had passed ashore, therefore he of necessity went over in the front. Skilfully concealed in the crowd, he narrowly watched the movements of the remaining passengers.

When her feet once touched the stones, Mrs. Chatwin felt as practical as the major. Anticipation was to a certain extent therewith turned into reality, and this lady was by no means constitutionally a dreamer only. A sense of overwhelming delight certainly assailed her as she passed on into the waiting-room which adjoined the custom-house, but it was essentially a practical delight, a healthy, physical sensation, altogether distinct from the roseate sunset emotion of an hour ago. It seemed to her that this was the first breath of the fulness of life that she had taken in all her twenty-seven years of existence, and she drew it deeply.

It was in this state of spiritual exaltation that in due course she passed out with the stream of passengers to experience the tender mercies of the dock officials, and just as she was countenancing the overtures of an obsequious, red-faced, red-whiskered man, with a brass label on his arm, with his 'Found your luggage, mum?' she observed Major Kennet hurry on in front of her. The task of selection was speedily accomplished, and a place at the counter obtained. Mrs. Chatwin's personal possessions numbered six, of which, after making the statutory inquiry, the officer selected two as tests,—of necessity the bulkiest and the most complex of lock and buckle. But this lady's fragrant secrets were rifled considerately, almost with respect, her indifferent good-humoured smile doubtless conducing to such liberal treatment. Hot altercations proceeded upon either hand, and in one of these Mrs. Chatwin became so engrossed that the brass-labelled porter had to recall her attention to the unlocked trunks. She then turned to secure them.

' I've taken the others on, ma'am,' remarked the man, seeing the lady glance about her.

' All right.   Is the train here?'

' Just outside, ma'am.'

Mrs. Chatwin followed the man with his truck, giving a last glance at the disputants she was leaving, and then confronted another scene. In the high confusion she recognised the infuriated features of Major Kennet lit up by the gaslight, backed by the luggage-van of a train, and opposed by several unwashed faces of the gross type peculiar to docks.

'I know you, you scoundrels,' he was shouting, as the lady drew near.   'I saw your winks. Guard, put those things in the van, do you hear, or I'll report you.   Drag 'em through the town, will you ?   No——'

To Mrs. Chatwin's supreme astonishment, she at once recognized her own half-dozen packages as the centre of the uproar.   As she came

up, the major checked his oaths, and vociferated,

‘Waterloo, madam?’

‘Yes, I am going to Waterloo.’

The guard was closing one half of the van
doorway, wholly oblivious of what was going
on. Mrs. Chatwin’s goods were piled upon a
hand-cart in the possession of two ragged out-
door adventurers who showed anxiety to start.
But the major physically arrested them, and
began to remove the luggage with his own
hand.

‘Get in, madam,’ cried he, excitedly—‘get
in, and I’ll see to these blackguards.’

After another glance at the situation, Mrs.
Chatwin deemed it wise to acquiesce, scarce
able, it is true, to restrain her laughter. The
major’s promptitude had evidently thwarted
a little plot, but her own buoyancy was such
that no humorous incident of travel could have
caused her much vexation. Had the men carried off her luggage to the town station, (which
the major’s words seemed to proclaim to be

their scheme,) and had she in consequence missed that particular train, it had been no catastrophe. She was in that state of high imaginative enthusiasm which only sees diversion in the petty adversities whence spring exasperation for the commonplace temper.

Seeing the device frustrated and no excessive gratuity in prospect, the guard for the first time became aware of the disagreement, and quickly brought the quarrel to an end. The major, assured of victory, smiled contemptuously at the volley of abuse to which he was subjected in hurrying to his place. 'Go to the devil, I tell you,' was all the satisfaction he vouchsafed to the threatening, importunate demands of the ragged volunteers, and at the door of his compartment he literally threw them off. He was just planted in his corner when there was a whistle and a shout, and the train moved onwards.

Major Kennet was not as a rule troubled with infirmity of purpose or the scruples of indecision generally, yet through the couple of hours' journey which was to bring him to Lon-

don he was strangely afflicted by both. He
bought a fresh paper at each station where the
train stopped, and it was flung on to the heap
beside him unopened. He was alone in the
carriage for the greater part of the way, so he
stood up, looked out into the dark, or walked
from end to end of the carpet like an animal
encaged. He would put light to a cigar, then
munch the tip obliviously, until awaking to the
vile effect upon his palate he would fling the
thing angrily from the window. The infernal
end had come, and he——but it should not.
At length he dozed uneasily until the stop at
Vauxhall finally aroused him. Then he found
that his mind was made up. He would, must
confront Mrs. Chatwin once more, come of it
what might. He stepped out at Waterloo as
though he had but come up from Bournemouth.

Unknown to the major, the lady herself was
seconding his resolution, but upon grounds far
enough removed from his own. It seemed to
her that common courtesy demanded some
acknowledgment of the service which Major
Kennet had rendered her, and on this account

she would permit one casual encounter on the station platform before their roads finally diverged. This divergence was the centre of the major's perplexity. He had suddenly discovered his unwillingness to arrange a day of which Mrs. Chatwin was not an essential part. The experience was a novel one, and presented a dilemma with which this gentleman was constitutionally not well fitted to deal. Beyond fifty though he was, he could not recall any personal precedent on such a point,—wherein, that is, considerations of his own convenience had found even a momentary serious dependence upon the movements or the existence of any other person. Whilst engaged with his luggage, Mrs. Chatwin came up to him, wearing her frankest, most fascinating smile. Major Kennet was conscious of a tremor before it.

'Oh, I'm so glad to catch you. Let me thank you so very much, Major Kennet.'

The gentleman seemed actually to hesitate in his ecstasy. He was prompted to remark jocularly upon her recovered good-humour, but his reason instantly checked him. When he did speak, it was merely a commonplace disclaimer that he permitted himself, coupled with an unnecessarily ardent scrutiny of the fair face before him. Mrs. Chatwin glanced at the luggage, and made some ingenuous reference to the joy of being *here* again ; then by another movement of her eyes adroitly gained the intervention of a porter.

'Yes, to a cab—that and that—this—that leather one—the next——'

Having indicated them all, she turned again to the major and held out her hand.

'Good-bye——'

'Good-bye, good-bye,' cried he, grasping her fingers. 'But we may meet again, you know. I cannot be content with a mere——'

'Possibly,' returned she, and was gone, whilst the major shuddered to hear Miss Felling's voice just beside him, talking about her luggage.

But he kept his back resolutely in that direction, until he left the place abruptly. His baggage remained there, and he went over towards the cabs. He had carefully noted the porter, and now met him with his empty truck.

'Where did that lady drive to?' asked the major, as he thrust half-a-crown into the man's hand.

'The Mettropole, sir.'

'Thank you.'

At his leisure, Major Kennet took a cab also.

END OF THE FIRST VOLUME.

London: Printed by Duncan Macdonald, Blenheim House, W.